PENGUINS AND MORTAL PERIL

MADIGAN AMOS ZOO MYSTERIES

RUBY LOREN

BRITISH AUTHOR

Please note, this book is written in British English and contains British spellings.

BOOKS IN THE SERIES

Penguins and Mortal Peril

The Silence of the Snakes

Murder is a Monkey's Game

The Peacock's Poison

A Memory for Murder

Whales and a Watery Grave

Chameleons and a Corpse

Foxes and Fatal Attraction

Monday's Murderer

Prequel: Parrots and Payback

PROLOGUE

The penguin enclosure was silent with the exception of a few of the younger ones getting chatty. The man in the enclosure raised a hammer and tapped away at a nail, fixing down a loose piece of board on the roof of the penguins' lodge. His mid-length, brown hair brushed his shoulders and curled up when he wiped a hand across his sweating forehead. The hole in the roof was hardly a priority. It was mid-July, but he was their keeper and he hated to think of them getting cold and wet in one of the summer storms that seemed to strike every few days in the South East of England. His dark green uniform was already faded from the amount of time he spent in the sun and his skin was tanned dark, accenting the carefree, surfer look that advancing age was only just beginning to tire.

The other keepers at the relatively small zoo had already gone home for the day. The zoo had officially closed almost three hours ago. Aquatic animals keeper and enthusiast, Ray Myers, was filling his time with little odd jobs, waiting for his helper to come. Then he could get started on the real reason he was working late that evening.

1

Penguins were brilliant creatures, but they were also pains in the butt, he reflected, thinking about the giant hole he'd found in the side of the pool. It didn't help that the pool hadn't been maintained as well as it should have been over the years. The penguins must have discovered a small weakness and made it bigger, the ancient fibreglass not proving much of an obstacle. Now he had some serious repair work on his hands that he hoped he'd manage to complete before the daylight faded.

He'd just finished testing his roof repairs when he heard the gate to the enclosure swing open. Ray winced, mentally adding the hideous shriek of the un-oiled hinges to his list of things to fix. He shook his head. Sometimes he thought he spent more time working as an odd job man than a zookeeper.

"Glad you made it. It'll be great having someone to pass me things. Slightly lessens the chance I'll do myself some serious mischief. I know I already told you what we're in for, but come and take a look for yourself. I can't believe what the little blighters managed before I noticed." Ray knelt down and leant over the ledge at the highest wall of the pool and pointed down. His helper got to his knees, too, his dark blue jeans taking on streaks of the dried dirt that scarcely held on to the ragged remnants of the plants Ray had once had put in, only for the penguins to destroy them. They really did have a penchant for destruction.

"That's a hell of a hole," his companion said, looking at the black chasm the size of a saucer. The waterline mark had been halfway up the hole, but it now sat below it.

Ray nodded. "Already had to drain the pool some to stop the leak. Now, I'm thinking that before I can patch it up, I'm gonna need to knock it through a bit more until I hit something that ain't rotten." He grimaced, his white teeth shining. "I'm a bit worried I'll knock in the whole damn pool until I find a good bit, so keep your fingers crossed. The board gave me permission to fix this up but they sure don't want to fork out for a new pool. Same old story about there not being enough money." Ray shook his head again as he climbed down over the ledge, precariously balancing on an ornamental rock. He stretched his other leg out and swung further so that it reached another rock, cemented in over the underwater viewing window. His face was pressed flat to the side of the pool, but if he moved both feet to the same rock and leant back as far as the fingers on his left hand would allow, he figured he'd be able to swing a hammer right for the hole.

"They should have let me do this when the zoo was still open. It would have been a great spectacle for all those kids to watch when I mess this up and take a dive into the pool." He eyed the top of the water with distaste. Oil from the penguins' most recent meal and their feathers floated along the surface giving it an iridescent quality. A penguin with yellow tufts sticking out from its head floated by below him and he tried to wave it away with a hand. He turned to throw his helper an exasperated look. "The last thing we need is for me to slip and fall on one of the little guys. You can bet those animal rights nuts would be all over it in a second." He shook his head once more as he felt around the jagged edges of the penguin made hole, feeling it crumble easily beneath the fingers of his right hand. "I don't know what the world is coming to. When will they get it into their empty heads that we're here to help the animals? The breeding programmes that we have here at Avery Zoo, and other zoos just like us, are what keeps many species from dying out for good. Why don't they understand that?"

His companion shrugged a little, knowing better than to try and contribute anything when Ray was on one of his trains of thought. There was a skeleton dressed as an ill-fated explorer who resided in the tunnel the zoo's little safari train chugged its way through. The staff liked to joke that Ray had talked him to death.

"Hey, shouldn't you get started?" the companion finally said in a gap between trains of thought.

Ray looked up and saw the sky starting to streak with pink as the sun sank lower. "You're right, you'd better hand me that sledgehammer. Time's a ticking!" he said, stretching a hand out to take it.

His helper returned carrying the heavy hammer but hovered on the edge for a moment. "Did you have a word with Mr Avery?"

Ray frowned for a second but then nodded. "Yeah, I did. He said that it was all okay but I shouldn't go chatting about it." His eyes creased up at the corners. "As if I'd do a thing like that."

"Well, that's a relief anyway," the helper said, stepping forwards with the hammer. Ray's fingers stretched out in anticipation as his companion got to his knees to avoid any danger of slipping over the edge and lifted the hammer up... away from the penguin keeper's grasping hand.

"Hey, what are you...?" Ray watched disbelievingly as the hammer was lifted high above his companion's shoulder, only for it to come crashing down on Ray's skull with a sickening thunk. Every muscle holding Ray in place on his precarious perch relaxed and he pitched backwards into the pool. His body twitched and turned as he returned to the surface. It floated face down with a red halo already spreading through the water.

His helper wiped the shaft of the heavy hammer on his dark polo shirt and after a moment's thought, flung the sledgehammer in after the body of the keeper. It landed with a loud splash, before sinking to the bottom of the pool. The penguins were already diving to investigate the new additions when he turned away and walked back towards the gate.

The penguin pool still glowed with light in the twilight of the evening and the helper automatically flipped the light switches off on his way out through the squeaky gate.

His heart hammered in his chest, as he made his way back through the quiet zoo. He avoided all of the areas that had cameras watching day and night - just as the boss had told him to. He felt sick with nerves and wondered if it was because of the terrible thing he'd done, or the fear of someone catching him now. His hanging hands clenched into fists. The job had been done and everything was going to be okay now, he reassured himself, as he exited the zoo through a side gate near the main entrance.

Glancing from side to side, he finally broke cover and stepped out into the grey, gravelled car park. A few cars remained over night, but he knew they all belonged to members of the board, who were presumably working away in their various offices, deciding the future of the zoo. His mouth twitched when he saw the familiar car park sign. It proclaimed that there was no CCTV, which meant the zoo wasn't responsible for anything that happened. He also hoped it would mean that no one would have noticed he'd stayed late that night. Just to be extra sure, he'd parked miles away from the main entrance, his pickup truck partially concealed behind the picnic barn.

On the drive back home he idly wondered what new joke the zoo staff would make about the skeleton in the tunnel.

THE FACE OF DEATH

I t was Saturday morning and I would only be five minutes into the working day before I figured out the weekend was not going to be a fun one.

The zoo hadn't even opened when I pulled up outside in my battered, dark blue Ford Fiesta, but that didn't stop me from being pounced upon as soon as I walked through the door of the staffroom. Dark-haired, despite being in his forties, and with a face made up of hard angles topped off with surprising blue eyes, Morgan Eversfield was quite the heart throb among the more mature members of staff at the zoo. Probably some of the younger ones, too - although, I definitely wouldn't count myself among the fan club. To me, Morgan was mostly a thorn in my side. This was due to him having the dubious privilege of being the zoo's animal welfare manager, which meant he was my boss.

"Madigan, you're just the person I was hoping to bump into," Morgan said. I immediately knew it was bad, as I was only the person he hoped to bump into when he wanted something. At any other time, I could have sworn that the man had some kind of supernatural powers of avoidance, especially when any of the zookeepers said the word 'budget'.

It was uncanny.

"What can I do for you, Morgan?" I pasted on my best Saturday morning smile, which mostly consisted of me baring my teeth at him. To his credit, he didn't recoil, which probably meant he *really* needed a favour.

"Ray's usually here at seven to do the early morning penguin feed, but it's half past, so I guess he's caught up in traffic." His fingers made quote marks in the air when he said the word 'traffic', temporarily changing the definition to 'hungover'. "You'll be able to fit feeding the penguins in on your morning round, won't you?"

It wasn't actually a question.

I wearily nodded, already feeling the day stretching out before me. If Ray didn't get here soon, I'd no doubt be saddled with the rest of his duties, too. That's what happened when the animals you specialised in looking after were the leftovers of the other keepers. Everyone assumed that you would be fine covering for anyone else, as you didn't apparently have a specific affiliation.

I glanced at my reflection in the smeary glass of the reptile enclosures as I walked by. The way my hair had refused to behave that morning should have been all the hint I needed that the day was unlikely to go my way. My normally sensible, shoulder length, natural blonde hair was taking a break from its usual waves and had decided that wild frizz was the latest thing. The bright yellow rimmed glasses I was wearing slid a little on my nose and I noted the rise in humidity wasn't exclusive to the reptile house.

A few monkeys whooped at me as I walked through the zoo on my way to the food store, but mostly things were quiet. Most animals were still sleeping... lucky them.

Working in the zoo had always been my dream job. I'd

been one of those little girls who was completely obsessed with animals. It had been enough to make my parents splash out on an expensive season pass to our local zoo, where I'd spent as much time as they'd let me. It had been at that zoo where I'd graduated from doing fun 'keeper for a day' kids experiences, to actually training as a keeper.

After qualifying, I'd worked at Avery Zoo in Gigglesfield for the past four years. I'd developed a habit of taking on any animal that the other keepers had shunned as being 'not their specialism'. It was in this way I had broadened my knowledge of animal care and had realised that in many cases, I could figure out when one of my charges was less than happy and intuitively know the solution. It wasn't a skill I'd particularly told anyone about, but I hoped that the results spoke for themselves. I wasn't surprised that a whole bunch of animals, who traditionally struggled to breed in captivity, were suddenly starting to reproduce at Avery Zoo.

The reminiscent smile slipped from my face, as I entered the store where all animal food was kept and slouched into the refrigerated area to fetch some fish. Two navy blue buckets had 'penguins' scrawled across them in permanent marker and I reluctantly picked them up, opening a large, watery bag of fish. The strong waft hit me immediately and I resigned myself to smelling the same, unpleasant smell all day long, as I would no doubt manage to slop some of the vile water on myself during the feeding frenzy.

Deciduous trees shielded the behind-the-scenes walkway that all of the keepers used to access the animal enclosures. It didn't escape my notice that there was neither hide nor hair of anyone else at work. Saturdays were notorious for staff arriving late, although Ray's half an hour tardiness was definitely pushing it.

The clamour of the penguins reached my ears long before I arrived at the gate outside their enclosure. I placed the buckets by my feet. My hand fumbled for the ring of keys I'd grabbed from the key board. The gate swung open when I attempted to slide the key in the lock. Hairs on the back of my neck stood up and a shiver jumped down my spine.

Something didn't feel right.

I tried to tell myself that Ray must have forgotten to lock the gate when he'd left at the end of yesterday, but I could see an assortment of tools and bits of wood, left strewn around near the penguins' lodge. I flicked on the lights that softly illuminated the penguin's pool for the benefit of the zoo's visitors.

It wasn't until I walked round the corner, buckets in hand, that I saw the body.

At first, my mind refused to accept what it was seeing. There was a dark shape at the bottom of the pool. The movement of the water, caused by a few of the smarter penguins swimming in anticipation of the fish being thrown in made it hard to see clearly. What I couldn't pretend to overlook was the familiar dark green polo shirt that the corpse was wearing and the way a cloud of brown hair floated back and forth with the currents. It looked like Ray wasn't caught up in traffic after all.

I glanced down at the buckets in my hands and concluded that I couldn't feed the penguins the usual way, by tossing the lot into the pool and making them do a little bit of work for their breakfast. A few head shakes later and I was pretty sure I was thinking more clearly. I dumped the buckets of fish on a relatively flat piece of concrete and let the penguins fight it out.

"Reception, hello?" I said into the walkie talkie that all zookeepers carried.

"Oh hey Madi, how are you doing? I was just thinking of calling for a chat."

I winced as Jenna Leary's nasal voice came across the

frequency. We were friends, but not really. She was the kind of girl who would compliment you to your face and then say the exact opposite the moment your back was turned. I shook those thoughts from my head and tried to focus. "There's a body at the bottom of the penguin pool. I think it's probably Ray, the penguin keeper."

"You're kidding! He's dead?"

"Unless he's just broken the world record for the longest time spent underwater without breathing, I'm going to say yes," I said, and then immediately regretted it when Jenna asked me to clarify if he was really dead or not. With hindsight, it probably was a little too soon for jokes.

"Just call the police and tell them someone's..." I hesitated. Murdered? Killed? "...had a fatal accident," I finished, figuring that was the safest option. A zookeeper had ended up at the bottom of the penguin pool and I doubted it was the penguins who had put him there. The tools and wood suggested that Ray had probably been doing repair work before something had happened and he'd wound up at the bottom of the pool.

I took a few steps closer to the edge of the water and could vaguely make out a smaller, darker shape, lying a few feet away from where Ray had come to rest.

A quick trip down to the underwater viewing window revealed a little more than I would have liked to see. It was Ray Myers all right. His eyes were still open and his head was turned towards the window, giving me the perfect view of his gaping mouth. His head was the wrong shape.

My gaze rested upon the other item at the bottom of the pool. It was a large sledgehammer. I joined the dots and was willing to bet that Ray's head had almost certainly come into contact with that hammer.

I don't know how I long I stood there, looking at the face of death, but it felt like an age had passed before I heard the fall of many feet and realised that the police had arrived. The next hour consisted of me sitting and waiting for the police to get around to asking their questions, or whatever it was they would want from me. Blue, police tape had gone up across the entrance to the penguin enclosure, blocking it from public access. It was something that I should have thought to do myself, but my mind was elsewhere.

I rubbed my ear, half listening to the discussions among the police as they discussed their theories about what had transpired. The sledgehammer had been recovered from the bottom of the pool. I'd overheard that it was strangely free from fingerprints, which apparently wouldn't wash off in water that quickly. A few greasy smears were all that had been uncovered.

That was when talk of a second person began.

"You're a zookeeper here, aren't you?" One of the police officers had turned my way and I realised I recognised him. It was Detective Rob Treesden. He often came into the zoo to run child safety workshops for the local school kids in one of the rooms we rented out for events.

It wasn't surprising that he didn't know who I was. I'd only ever known him by sight, but Jenna had a tendency to go on about him for weeks after he'd run one of his workshops.

I looked at his tanned face, noting the deep crows feet at the corner of each eye and the way the skin at his jaw was just starting to sag and become jowly. To his credit, he possessed two bright blue eyes that looked like chips of aquamarine and a full-head of salt and pepper hair, but I still thought he was way too old to be considering a date with. Jenna had a thing for older men. And younger men. And any men in-between those parameters.

I realised the detective was still waiting for an answer, so I nodded in response.

"Could you tell me how you came to find the deceased?" he asked.

I gave an account of my brief day at work, while he wrote it all down.

"Do you think it was an accident?" I asked when he'd closed his notebook and seemed to be done with questions. He fixed me with a look from those vivid, blue eyes.

"We won't know for sure what happened until we've reviewed all of the facts," he said. That was definitely code for 'it's none of your business'.

I nodded slowly and turned to go. It was clear I wasn't needed or wanted in the area any more. Plus, there were animals that needed feeding and checking on and I was not naive enough to hope that any of the other keepers would have taken on my duties after they'd heard I'd been caught up. All of Ray's aquatic animals were probably now my responsibility, too. I mentally waved goodbye to my lunch break.

It was only when I walked back through the gate, empty buckets in hand, that something important occurred to me.

"Detective," I called, and the salt and pepper policeman turned from his discussion with barely concealed annoyance. "I turned the penguin pool lights on when I got here this morning. Someone must have turned them off last night."

"Could Mr Myers have turned them off before he started work?" the detective asked, now a little less annoyed.

I thought about it. "No, he'd have no reason to. They get turned off overnight but he'd have wanted to do whatever fixing he was planning on doing while it was still light. If he was here as late as twilight, the lights probably would have helped him to see. Especially if he was working on the pool itself." I nodded towards the crime scene photographer, who was leaning over the high side of the pool, photographing a jagged hole in the side. I was guessing the police had deduced that this was probably what Ray had been trying to fix when the fatal accident had occurred.

I frowned a little as I finally made it beyond the gate. Had it been an accident? If you paired the lack of fingerprints on the mallet with what I'd noticed about the light switch, it did start to look like Ray hadn't been here alone last night. Had the other person present panicked and tried to cover it up when disaster had struck, or was it no accident at all that Ray Myers had ended up at the bottom of the penguin pool?

I found myself back at the food store and tried to put the events of the morning behind me. I had several aquariums full of fish I didn't know how to feed to deal with and then there was my usual odds and ends round. Capybaras, echidnas, lemurs, porcupines, and wallabies, the list just went on and on. I knew by the time I'd finished breakfast it would be time to start the evening feed.

Already the stress of the day was mounting up, and by the time I'd thrown the fruit and veg in the general direction of the lemurs, I was almost tempted to snag some for myself. My stomach was growling and my mood was heading south. That was why I nearly bit off Tiffany's head.

"Hi, you look like you're working hard," she said, appearing from nowhere carrying a box of stuffed animals.

Tiffany Wallace had been my friend ever since I started work at the zoo. She was just a shop assistant back then, but had since risen up to be manager of commerce. Technically, that made her a little above my pay grade but with someone who possessed as much natural charm as Tiff, it never got in the way. Naturally blessed with unusual strawberry blonde hair, her skin was unfairly flawless and usually took on a light gold hue, despite her hair's colouring. Slender and tall, she turned heads anywhere she went and still managed to stay well-grounded.

It was enough to make you sick.

"All work, no play," I said, with a touch more bitterness than I'd intended.

Tiff must have noticed because her smile slipped for all of a millisecond before she bounced back. "Oh, of course, how could I? You'll have heard about Ray Myers, the penguin keeper," she carried on, sensitivity permeating her voice while she automatically made an allowance for my snappish behaviour.

"I was the one who found him," I admitted, surprised that it wasn't common knowledge. The power of the rumour mill at the zoo usually meant everyone knew when something had happened what felt like mere seconds after it had occurred.

Tiff's mouth turned into a perfect 'o'. "Are you serious? It was you who found him? Jenna made it sound as though she was the one who…" She trailed off and threw me a bemused smile.

I managed to return it. "That figures," I said, thinking about Jenna. At the same time, I was kind of glad she was taking the credit and any resulting limelight. With the amount of work I had to do, being bombarded with questions was not going to speed along my day.

"Hey, did you hear anyone mention that they stayed to help Ray out last night?" I asked.

Tiff threw me a sharp-eyed look. "I think I heard Tom say that he remembered Ray mentioning staying late to fix a hole in the penguin pool. A couple of the workmen on site saw him before they clocked off at the end of the day yesterday, but none of them mentioned seeing anyone else. Do the police think that… he had company?" Tiff tactfully probed.

"I don't know what they've concluded but I'm pretty sure someone else was there." I thought back to the way Ray's head had looked and that big, heavy hammer, which I was sure had been the cause of his demise. Would somehow dropping it on his own head have caused that level of damage, or had the scene just been arranged that way to help the police draw the simplest conclusion?

"I hope the police interview those animal rights crazies. They make me feel so uncomfortable. It's like they think I'm a criminal," Tiff said, following my own line of thought.

The 'animal rights crazies' were a rag tag bunch of protesters, who were currently camped outside the zoo entrance. Every day they'd be there waving their signs and shouting about alleged animal abuse taking place in the zoo. Some months, the group dwindled or even evaporated entirely, as the activists presumably found more pressing animal abuse allegations to take a stand against. Unfortunately, a recent incident at the zoo had drawn them back and they'd come like bees to honey. Or rather, flies to the stinking heap of dung that was the zoo's unwanted PR leak.

"I can't really see why they'd do something like this though," I said, carefully. "To go from waving signs around outside a zoo and shouting abuse at employees to murder is quite a leap."

Tiff's blue and gold eyes darkened for a second and she lowered her voice to a whisper. "Yes, but I've heard rumours that another group is coming here. People who have a reputation for taking matters further."

My dark, and rather unruly, eyebrows shot up. It was the first I'd heard of more extreme activists. What if they'd already arrived?

Tiff absentmindedly flicked her hair back over her shoulder and at least three dads in the near vicinity tried not to openly drool. "I should let you get on, but I'll be sure to tell you if I hear anything else." Tiff tended to hear all of the best gossip because everyone loved talking to her. I was never quite sure why she'd picked me out to be her best friend, but there was seldom a day when I wasn't grateful for it.

She sashayed off with her box of stuffed animals, leaving me to give the lemurs a once over. It wouldn't be long before I'd be back with their second feed.

I spared a moment to sit down after I'd fed the wallabies. Taking some time out with bouncy marsupials was actually justifiable. It was only one month ago that Gina and Lowry, two of my favourite wallabies, had given birth. Now bulges were just beginning to show in their respective pouches. The vet was pleased with their progress but I still liked to hang out with the pair of mummy wallabies, just to check. More than once I'd had a gut feeling about something being wrong with an animal. I'd long since learned to go with those gut feelings, as you never knew when it could be the difference between life and death... or even a new life coming into existence.

I thought about the echidnas, Alan and Joan, who had surprised the world last year by hatching three puggles in a first for a UK zoo in decades. That same other sense had whispered in my ear months beforehand that the echidnas needed more variety in their enclosure. I'd managed to convince the managers to add a running stream of water that led to a shallow pool. I'd also landscaped the enclosure on several levels to give the pair more hidey-holes and inter-esting places for little echidnas to investigate. It hadn't been long after, that they'd used the hollow tree log as a nesting site and the puggles had emerged, as healthy and happy as their parents.

Of course, the animal rights people had been furious. An incredulous smile formed on my lips. While animals were my life, I had no great love for the odd bunch who hung out every day in front of the entrance and generally did their very best to make a nuisance of themselves. They claimed to be animal lovers, but I'd always thought if they were truly that worried about the welfare of animals, they'd be doing something positive toward it. They could volunteer, or get a career that allowed them to have some say over the animal issues they particularly cared about. Instead, they spent their time harassing those who were actually trying to make difference.

I pursed my lips, as I thought over my very unpopular opinion. While I knew the majority of staff working at the zoo would most likely agree with me, pretty much no one would be stupid enough to say it out loud. You never knew who was listening and if recent events were anything to go by, someone was definitely telling tales to the other side.

I smiled and waved at Vanessa, the keeper who looked after the zoo's insect, reptile and amphibian collection. If it was slithery or slimy, Vanessa liked it. Vanessa looked at me over the rims of her winged glasses and bared her teeth, which I'd grown to assume was what passed as a smile for her. She disappeared through the heavy plastic flaps that separated the outside world from the muggy interior of the insect house.

Vanessa was one of the most experienced keepers at the zoo, but she was a little hard to swallow at times. I had no problem with her fondness for the creepy and the crawly, but her suggestions of more interactive exhibits weren't to everyone's taste. Most notably, her suggestion for an experience where people could walk among hornets and killer bee. It often made me wonder if she didn't secretly harbour hopes of an invertebrate world-takeover. Fortunately, the zoo board of directors shared my (and pretty much everyone else's) scepticism. They were also in charge of the zoo's insurance, which unsurprisingly wouldn't stretch to cover deaths from hornets and killer bees caused by an 'interactive' exhibit. That hadn't stopped Vanessa from resubmitting her proposal at every opportunity with a few slight modifications. I had heard hints that this summer's concept would be swimming with snakes... but only the venomous ones.

Gina's furry wallaby head nudged my cheek and I was snapped back to the reality of my double duty. I pulled the timetable I'd hastily printed off in-between maniacally throwing food at various animals. Every animal had been fed their first meal of the day, despite some of them loudly protesting my tardiness. Now it was time to see to some of the other pressing jobs and I noted with a sinking heart that the penguin pool wasn't the only bit of maintenance work Ray had been planning for the week.

The beavers' dam had grown to such a size that it was a hazard, both to the beavers who had little clue about the flaws of the zoo's artificial landscaping, and to the zoo's structure. The deep pool of water they'd created by damming up the stream that ran through their enclosure had grown exponentially since they'd managed to fully dam up the stream. Now it was in danger of flooding out of their enclosure and through the non-water sealed viewing window. I rolled my eyes at this oversight. Sabotaging the beavers' dam wasn't a task I relished. I knew it amounted to deliberately making work for the animals, but who was I to argue with the gods of health and safety?

Armed with some beaver treats, waders, and a broom, I squelched into the enclosure. Once the beavers were suitably distracted and out of harm's way, I set about poking holes in their dam and knocking off the topmost layer. There were plenty of trees and rocks in the enclosure, placed there for the very purpose of dam building, so I didn't expect it to be long before this job would need doing again. By the time I'd slunk out of the enclosure, the beavers' 'eeh' sounds of outrage were already filling my ears, as they discovered my subterfuge.

I hoped they didn't hold grudges.

Although I wouldn't have claimed it was my lucky day by any stretch of the imagination, the rest of the afternoon passed without anything else significant going wrong. It wasn't long before I'd finished the evening feed and found it was only one hour after my official finishing time.

I returned the last set of plastic bowls to the food store, but didn't exit back into the main zoo. Instead, I walked through into the main storeroom, where we kept large quantities of any food that could be stored for a length of time. Dry food and freezers full of all sorts of emergency supplies (in case anything ever happened to cut the zoo off) filled what was essentially a miniature warehouse. I reached exterior door, where deliveries were made, and used my keys to open it. Usually, keys for this door were kept back in the office and only used for deliveries, but this task meant I had been permitted special dispensation.

As well as looking after exotic animal species, the zoo had some behind-the-scenes residents that I liked to check on. There was a hay barn a little way behind the zoo, sitting on the field the warehouse backed on to. The larger, grass-eating animals were often put out to graze in these fields, but I was here to visit our only furry members of staff.

No one remembered when the cats had arrived. It was inevitable when you had a zoo full of animals with lots of food stored and left lying around by the animals that you had the rat problem to go with it. That was what had attracted the cats. Since they'd appeared, the zoo had always semi-looked after them, providing ample food to keep them going in case they had a bad night's hunting. I liked to think that whoever's job it had been to look after them before I arrived had also kept an eye on their health and taken any that looked to be in the wars to the vet. Just like any family, the cats didn't always get along, especially as they were a constantly changing group. Sometimes a tomcat or two would wander in and I would be responsible for scraping the loser off the floor the day after the fight to get seen to by the vet. After having their war wounds patched up, the toms would also wake up missing a couple of things. Thus, hopefully curbing both their natural male cat aggression and their ability to produce unwanted litters.

It wasn't always this easy. Often a feral cat with a grievous injury could still be the devil to catch. These weren't house pets, they were wild animals and I had the scars to prove it.

"Evening everyone," I said, entering the barn carrying the bowls of kitty chow. There was an immediate panicked scuffle as the cats on the barn floor retreated to the safety of the hay bales. A few of the more confident ones stared at me balefully from their spots up in the eaves of the barn. I rolled my eyes. I'd been feeding them for years and they still liked to pretend I was on a mission to poison them. "Believe me, if that were the case, I'd have used something much faster acting," I muttered in the direction of one of the bigger, ginger tom cats who I'd had many unhappy encounters with. He had a tendency to take on any male challenger, or apparently any cat that even looked at him the wrong way. I'd dragged him kicking screaming to be neutered, but it hadn't done anything to curb his bloodlust.

A furtive movement caught my eye and I turned in time to see a small black cat slink away after the others. She was slower moving for a good reason.

"Oh no," I breathed. I observed the way her belly hung a little low as she trotted between the bales of hay and managed to jump, relatively spryly, over one of the bales at the rear of the barn. From the brief glance I'd seen, I suspected she probably still a had a good few days to go before she popped, but I'd have to keep an eye on her in case the vet needed to be called out. I sighed. The vet would have to be called anyway. After momma cat had had her kittens and they were grown enough to be weaned, they'd all need to be caught and brought in to be neutered. Otherwise we'd have an epidemic of kittens on our hands in no time.

I frowned, not recognising the slight black cat with her distinctive white socks. New additions to the barn weren't uncommon. I wondered if this cat was an ex-pet who'd run off and got pregnant and was now about to pay for her little taste of freedom. I felt like the parent of a reckless teenager.

"Now you're going to have to accept the consequences of your actions, little missy," I said to her, in mock bossy tone. I would have to keep a close watch on the other cats, too, to make sure there wasn't an un-neutered tom around who might threaten her kittens. The others were usually okay with little ones. This wasn't the first rogue momma cat I'd seen crawl into the barn. I suspected they came because they knew there was food and shelter to be had here.

I placed the bowls down and turned to go, knowing it would be bedlam the moment I left the barn. Around thirteen pairs of eyes watched as I turned the corner, ready to strike the moment they knew I was really, definitely gone.

How's that for gratitude? I thought with a smile.

2

COMICS AND CREEPERS

Two days later, the police returned and the zoo rumour mill practically exploded.

While I was one of the police's first ports of call, I was not a contributor to gossip, but that didn't stop everyone from finding out why the police were back at the zoo. Detective Treesden caught me when I was finishing up cleaning out the porcupines' enclosure. It was another sunny day and the work was hot, so I wasn't at my most charming.

"Good morning, Ms Amos. We have a few more questions we need to ask in order to further our enquiries," Treesden said from the visitors' pathway.

I stepped out of the porcupine enclosure and came round to meet him, horribly aware that I smelt like manure and dirt. "What can I do to help you?" I asked, summoning up my public persona. I wondered if the seasoned detective could tell at a glance how fake it was.

Probably.

"As you are aware, we are looking into the unfortunate death of Mr Ray Myers. We have decided to treat this as a suspicious death, which is why I need to clarify a few things."

I nodded numbly, taking in what he'd just said. I'd known deep down that Ray hadn't just slipped and dropped that hammer on his head, despite someone perhaps wanting the police to think that. The light switch being turned off and the sheer amount of damage that had been inflicted on Ray's skull with that killing blow...

I looked up, suddenly realising that the detective had been speaking and I'd missed every word.

"Sorry, could you say that again?"

The detective sighed, but obliged. "How well did you know Mr Myers?"

I half-shrugged. "Everyone knows each other here at the zoo. Although, because of the different animals we work with, the other keepers can actually be the people we see the least of. All of us get together and have meetings every week, but I mean on a day-to-day basis," I carefully explained and then realised I hadn't really addressed the question. "Ray was a good guy. I know he was popular with a lot of the ladies here at the zoo and even dated a couple of them for a while." I watched as the detective started to scribble in his note book. "He was always nice to me and whenever we met in the food or supply store we'd have a friendly chat, usually about how things were going with our animals. He had a real thing about anything aquatic and was always lobbying for the zoo to get seals." I suppressed a grin. "I think he'd have asked for killer whales and dolphins, too, if he thought he'd be in with a shot, but we're just a small zoo and some animals simply don't do well in captivity," I added, thinking about the recent horrors that had been publicised on the TV.

At times it was difficult working as a zookeeper. You loved the animals you worked with, but you also knew that you were taking away from their natural environment and there would always be something missing for them. For some it was worse than others. That was why I liked the smallness of Avery zoo. The animals we had here had some really great habitats and weren't cramped by any means. On the flip side, it was sometimes necessary to keep animals in zoos, both for education and to protect them from the destruction that other humans were currently wreaking on natural habitats and native populations.

"...Ms Amos?" the detective said, and I realised I'd zoned out again. I shook my head and he repeated himself. "Where were you on Friday evening, the night the deceased died?"

"I went home after work, cooked dinner, and stayed in to draw... some stuff." I cleared my throat, not wanting to share too much with the detective, who almost certainly wouldn't care anyway.

"Is there anyone who can vouch for your whereabouts?"

I blinked. "Hang on, am I a suspect?" I asked, first feeling annoyed and then incredulous.

"We're just exploring all of the possible avenues," Treesden told me in a toneless voice, presumably intended to placate.

I raised a brown eyebrow and folded my arms. "I suppose I should be flattered that you think a five foot zero woman could batter a man the size of Ray to death with a hammer." I paused and thought about it some more. "Or that I'd have been able to get close enough to him to do it without him suspecting anything. If there is a killer, they were probably there to help Ray out, so he wouldn't have expected the attack and fought back." It was an interesting idea, I thought to myself. I hadn't noticed any signs of a struggle when I'd had the unfortunate experience of coming face to face with Ray's corpse.

The detective made a tiny note in his book. "We're just exploring..."

"...all of the possible avenues," I parroted back. Maybe it

was the heat, but my public persona was well past its use by date.

The detective raised his eyes from his notebook just long enough to look me up and down, but I could tell he was just internally concluding I was probably not the killer. My lack of bulging biceps (and motive) were hopefully more than enough to convince him of that.

I wasn't about to share it, but I was actually pretty strong, despite being on the small side. As a zookeeper, you were pretty much on your own when it came to dealing with what needed to be done for the animals. Heavy lifting was a big part of that, no matter what the zoo's health and safety officer liked to believe.

"I believe I've asked all my questions at this time, unless there are any amendments you'd like to make to your original statement?" he asked, one dark eyebrow, not yet grey streaked, raised in query.

I shook my head. Everything I'd told them had been the truth. Nothing else had come to mind in the days that had passed since I'd found Ray in the penguin pool.

"Someone will be in touch if we have any further questions. Thank you for your time," he added and I privately noted that his public persona was about as genuine as mine was today.

I returned to the porcupine enclosure to finish off the sweeping. I hadn't been back at it long when someone called good morning to me.

Lucy Bond, the keeper in charge of the zoo's few larger cats, and some of the other mixed bag of mammals, waved her fingers energetically at me. She had blonde hair trimmed in a pixie cut and clear blue eyes she liked to emphasise with black kohl so thick, it almost looked ancient Egyptian inspired. Her zookeeper's green polo shirt still looked as though she'd got it new from the packet yesterday and I'd been meaning to ask her how she kept it looking so fresh.

I smiled and raised my own hand to wave back, feeling I should really make the effort for Lucy. She was one of the friendlier, less weird, keepers, but there was another reason why I was putting on my best face for her.

While the feral cats I'd taken to looking after did keep the worst of the rat problem at bay, the board had deemed one month ago that it wasn't enough. Visitors had begun to report seeing rats running through enclosures and even on the visitor walkways. With customer approval ratings down, the board made the unpopular decision to poison the rats. I'd spoken against this measure to the board, being seriously worried that one of the feral cats would find and eat a poisoned rat.

As far as the zoo was concerned, what actually happened was much, much worse.

Eventually the board had conceded that the poison would have to be very fast acting and would only be placed in areas that the cats weren't able to access. This stipulation had been unpopular with certain board members, but it had been the unhappy compromise most agreed was both effective and safe. Unfortunately, it didn't work out that way.

The poison was placed and various members of staff collected a few dead rodents in the days that followed. I monitored the cats in the barn and was relieved to find they were all fine. The directors were just about to chalk the operation up as a success, and most likely start pushing to have the poison in the areas I'd asked them to avoid.

Then the serval died.

It happened so quickly, there was only one report of the animal being unwell. A visitor said they thought they'd seen the spotted cat vomiting but by the time Lucy had arrived to investigate, Kiota the serval was already dead.

An autopsy performed by the vet had uncovered half-digested rat and confirmed the presence of poison in the serval's system. No one had a clue as to how the rat could have gotten into the serval's enclosure, but that was the problem with rats, they could get in absolutely anywhere.

After the serval had died, the zoo had acted quickly, cordoning off the area from the public and then waiting with bated breath for the next few days after the incident. Nothing was reported to the papers or written online. The board assumed that they'd acted fast enough and that no one outside of the zoo knew about the accident. But secrets are hard to keep, even in a small zoo.

One week later, the protesters turned up in full force. Somehow they knew every single detail about what had happened to the hapless serval. The group condemned the zoo for poisoning the rats and demanded that visitors boycott Avery and call for punishment to be dealt to the zoo.

If anything, the publicity the protesters generated reminded people that the zoo existed and visitor numbers went up, but it wasn't all good news. Every visitor had to run the gauntlet past the anti-social protesters and no public attraction wants a group of people hanging around outside, yelling about something you'd rather was swept under the rug.

It had been five days since the activists had turned up and the board had launched a full investigation. Actually, they'd launched two full investigations. One was into the circumstances surrounding the demise of the serval. That was the one pushed to the public and the protesters. The other investigation was internal, as the board went in search for the source of the leak.

Neither investigation had turned up much actual evidence yet, but the latter was turning sour. The zoo relied on volunteers to help with the day-to-day running of the zoo. They did jobs like guiding the public through the insect house, or monitoring our interactive lemur walk. Some of them did it in order to boost their chances of being employed in an animal related job, but others performed their roles, simply because they loved animals. Unfortunately, this was the group of people that the board of directors suspected were the source of the leak. Whilst knowledge of the serval's death was supposed to be restricted to employees only, staff often didn't discern between paid members and volunteers, so everyone that was involved with the zoo had heard about the tragedy.

The volunteers had their own Facebook group and a group chat. It was this chat that the board were insisting upon being given access to. This demand had not gone down well with the majority of the volunteers. The board seemed to think it was because they were protecting the source of the leak. I thought it was far more likely that some of the volunteers' managers, and even members of the board, were discussed in the group chat and I was betting not everything was polite.

The ghost of a smile crossed my lips while I finished up the last of the sweeping. It was lucky that the zookeepers weren't prone to conversing on social media. I thought about the number of real life conversations I'd had, filled with disparaging remarks about whichever manager was being pigheaded. If the volunteers shared the same opinions as the zoo's staff, I'd be pretty reluctant to let the directors pick apart what was supposed to be a private conversation.

I returned the broom I'd been using to the supplies store and ditched the wheelbarrow full of dirty bedding onto the vast compost heap, on the edge of the fields. If the board carried on treating the volunteers with suspicion, it wouldn't be long before the zoo didn't have any volunteers left. Despite directors often overlooking the volunteers, they were actually essential to keep the basically understaffed zoo ticking along. If they wanted to get rid of the volunteers, they'd have to employ some more people.

I imagined the expressions on the directors' faces if they were told they needed to spend more money and rolled my eyes. They could do with treading lightly in their investigation.

While I worked, theories popped in and out of my head. I wondered if Ray's death was somehow tied up with the poisoning incident. Had one of the activists caught the keeper alone, only for the confrontation to turn violent? Alternatively, what if someone had suspected that Ray himself was responsible for the leak and had taken their loyalty to the zoo a little too far? He'd had a reputation for being a chatterbox. I rubbed my slightly freckled chin, not able to piece together anything more than multiple hypotheses. I shrugged my shoulders and mentally moved on to the next task. It was the police's job to do the figuring out.

My next stop of the day was to check in on a couple of the larger animals at the zoo, the capybaras. Currently, they weren't the happiest bunch. In a rare, money-spending move, instigated by me, the board had concluded that the capybaras' enclosure needed updating. What exactly those updates entailed, I wasn't yet sure. Despite offering to design it myself, outside experts had been hired to create the concepts. I was curious to see what it would look like when finished. Unfortunately for the short term, I had a group of capybaras squashed into a non-public enclosure, only ever intended to hold otter adolescents. It had a tiny pool and not much vegetation was left, due to a lack of upkeep and the surprisingly spontaneous decision to update.

Melancholy was written all over the faces of Doris and Louis when I arrived by the inadequate enclosure.

"Come on guys, it won't be long before your new place is

all done and I'm sure it's going to be great," I told them, when I walked in with a bowl of snacks. The capybaras didn't even look up.

The pair had been placed together a couple of years ago. Since then, they'd disappointingly never managed to reproduce, although I had a sneaking suspicion that this was one of the reasons why the board had agreed to make changes. Baby animals attracted visitors, especially if those babes were cute, furry, and relatively uncommon. They were hoping for a rerun of the echidnas' success.

I placed the bowl of snacks down and looked at the remains of their virtually untouched breakfast. Concern lined my face as I gave the pair the once over. They were definitely looking a little on the skinny side. I shook my head. They'd better get a move on with the enclosure, or there'd be another animal crisis to deal with. I bit my lip, sorry to have even had the thought. If these animals were really in trouble, it was my job to do something to help them.

"Don't worry, I'll have a word with the builders and see if I can't kick their butts a little harder and get you back where you belong in no time," I promised, smiling as I saw Doris take a tentative sniff at the fruit snack I'd brought and then eat a piece.

It was a start.

The builders had started work on the capybara enclosure last week, right before all of the drama had kicked off. Despite the constantly cited budget limitations, the group of builders were often at the zoo, whether it was to overhaul enclosures, build new exhibits, or extend the ever-growing adventure play area. Over the years, I'd learnt the names of all of the regulars.

When I arrived at the building site, the first change I noticed was the enlargement. A small outside pathway, that had once led to a now obsolete viewing window for the macaws' sleeping area, had been flattened, along with the old boundary fence. The capybaras' pool had also been smashed up. At the moment, there wasn't much to see but rubble, and I hoped it was closer to completion than it looked. Otherwise the unhappy intended recipients might start to waste away.

"Hi," I said, approaching one of the builders named Gary, who had stopped to crack open a bottle of coke. He turned his incredibly tanned face and then looked away again, giving me a view of his hairy neck. His brown, wavy hair was kept close to his head and his watery eyes seemed unfocused to me. Perhaps that was just because I wasn't Tiff, I thought in a rare moment of jealousy.

"I was just wondering if I could see the plans for this enclosure? I'm a zookeeper here," I felt I had to clarify, as he wasn't exactly giving me major recognition signs.

Gary turned back once he realised I was talking to him and half shrugged. "Yeah, sure, they're right over there." He nodded towards a collection of gear that had been dumped and I caught a glimpse of some dirt streaked pieces of paper.

"Thanks," I said, as enthusiastically as he deserved. I walked over and picked up the pieces of paper.

Being the zookeeper tasked with looking after the capybaras, the original concepts had actually been run by me, but I knew there was always a big difference between what was conceptualised and what actually happened. I looked down at the sheets and noted that the plans for the enlarged, capybara-friendly plant filled pool and the feeding stream had stayed much the same. However, some key elements had been altered, or perhaps they'd not even been confirmed when I'd been shown the ideas. I frowned at the sparse, clearly trendy, landscaped area that made up most of the enclosure.

"Hey!" I called to the largest group of workers, who were slinging pieces of shattered concrete into wheelbarrows with spades. They stopped working as I walked, or rather stomped, over to them. "You see this..." I pointed to the plans. "Is this all that's going to be added? A few ornamental trees? These animals need cover and variety to keep them happy and healthy, not a designer garden!"

Two builders, Jack and Todd, exchanged a glance and then looked to their boss, Rich - a man I'd never managed to see eye-to-eye with. My ever so slightly raised voice had attracted attention. Two zookeepers I hadn't even noticed strolled over to join our little group.

"What's up, Madi?" Tom, the keeper in charge of the zoo's primate collection, walked over and nodding his sandy head towards me. Colin, an older keeper who looked after the equine and hoofed animals, merely grunted - but that was pretty good going for Colin.

"I was looking at these plans and noticed that there's hardly any planting and hardly any cover for Doris and Louis. I know they need more plants and, quite frankly, more interest. While this may make them easier to spot for the visitors, I know it's not the best that can be done for them," I said, feeling sure that I was right. It was that sensation in my gut - the one I always got which whispered to me in an inner voice, *you can make this better.*

Tom barely glanced at the plans and shrugged. "What can you do? The board hired an expert. I'm sure they know what they're talking about, far more than we mere mortals," he said, but I didn't get major 'we're all in this together' vibes from him.

"But it could be so much better! I could even draw in the changes myself. It wouldn't be that hard and I doubt it would even cost much more. We could just add a few levels to stop the monotony and then put in shrubs and other plants here, and a grazing plateau here..." I pointed as each idea occurred to me but when I raised my head, I was surrounded by glazed expressions everywhere except…

My gaze collided with a pair of dark eyes that looked curiously back into my own. There was something steady in that look, something that spoke of authority. I didn't recognise the man those eyes belonged to.

"It is what it is," Tom was saying, while the builders mindlessly parroted back the same sentiments.

"New guy?" I said, tilting my head in the direction of the man who'd just picked up the handles of a fully-laden wheelbarrow. His hair was dark, short at the sides and longer on top, in a fashionable, but smart, cut. His arms were perfectly bronzed and I could see the thick knots of muscles that contracted when he started to push the heavy load. A generic, dark, tribal tattoo peeked out below his sleeve, midway up his bicep. Somehow it didn't seem to fit with everything else.

"Yeah, we needed a couple of extra guys to fill in on this job. That's Lowell, he's just joined the company." Rich, my least favourite builder, smiled indulgently. "He's picking things up okay. I'm sure he'll be up to speed with us all in no time." The men around him chuckled.

I tried not to raise my eyebrows. I'd gotten one look at Lowell before he'd walked away to dump the rubble, but even in that small window of time I'd noticed there was something different about him. I snapped out of my thoughts only to realise that the men were doing some eyebrow raising of their own.

"You're not the first one to ask about him. I really don't know why everyone's got their knickers in a twist," Rich said, and the others sniggered behind their hands.

I felt my cheeks turn pink and cursed my treacherous skin for this obvious display. Why couldn't I be Tiffany's gorgeous shade of gold and never ever blush? Instead, I was stuck with pale skin that simply gained more freckles in lieu of a tan, when exposed to the sun. People that were interested in being nice to me, like a few close relatives, would say my colouring was that of an English rose. I'd often done all I could to get rid of it, up to and including a disastrous spray tan. Pale gold was just another unreachable goal.

"I guess I'll put my thoughts to the directors," I said, in a halfhearted attempt to show that I wasn't willing to back down and go away.

The builders just shrugged and went back to their business.

Out of the corner of my eye, I saw Tom and Colin exchange a knowing smirk and I wished that my height was just a little more imposing. Just sometime, it would be nice to not be considered cute when I was at my angriest. Part of me wanted to do something to wipe the smirks from their faces, but I'd been working with Colin for years, and Tom for several months. I knew it was a lost cause. The only way to win would be to sneak the changes I wanted through by tactical manoeuvring. I chewed my lip and resolved to think of a cunning plan later.

The sun was still beating down when I walked back through the zoo, my mind firmly fixed on lunch break. I was still doing most of Ray's job, but fortunately Morgan, our manager, had stepped in and divvied up the duties a little more fairly. He wasn't going to win the 'Mr Popularity' award from the other keepers, but I was grateful.

"Hey Madi!" A slightly strained voice called.

I looked to my right and noticed Leah struggling beneath the weight of a potted, box plant. I rushed over to help lift the terracotta pot, following the relieved instructions of the other zookeeper, as we manoeuvred the plant pot into place next to a solid fence, that came up to my stomach. The other keeper wiped a hand across her dark skin and fluffed out her wild curls, which had a hint of red to them.

"Thanks a million. I really thought I was going to drop it," she said. I looked pointedly at her well-defined arm muscles, feeling that I hadn't exactly been the deciding factor.

"Are you decorating for the summer?" I asked, looking properly at the box plant, which had been clipped into a spiral shape.

Leah shook her head and leant on the fence. "Nope, I'm hoping that placing plants here will discourage parents from dropping their kids over the other side of the fence. I mean, there's a double fence here for a reason." She gestured over the top of the solid wooden barrier to the second fence that ran around the perimeter of the enclosure. "It's a couple metres away from the other fence for a good reason, but no, they always drop their little ones down for a closer look and then complain when they get bitten." Drawn by her voice, an enquiring neck poked out from behind a bush, followed by a pair of long legs as the emu approached.

"Don't give me that look, I know you pretend to be all friendly and interesting until some parent drops their little darling close enough for you to peck." The emu blinked and Leah frowned. "Count yourself lucky there's no legislation that says birds need to be put down after biting someone! Although, that's probably because there'd be no birds left, if someone decided to pass that law." She waggled her eyebrows and I threw a sideways look at the emu in question.

I knew his sneaky ways all too well. I'd agreed to cover for Leah when she'd gone on holiday. Boris (so called due to the blonde feathers that stuck up all over his head) liked to wait until your back was turned then sneak up and bite you from behind, before running away when you tried to swat him. He was also a shameless thief and had managed to steal my dinosaur purse before beating another hasty retreat. I'd made quite the spectacle of myself chasing him around the enclosure, until he'd abandoned my purse in favour of the small child who'd just been dropped over the outer fence.

"You do have a point," I admitted, looking at the various plants and noting how some possessed thorns. "I hope it works out and Boris' biting days are over."

Leah pulled a sympathetic face at Boris who stared back with his beady eyes. "Just look at that face though. I know he's going to be miserable if it works," she sighed. "Oh well, at least it looks like the zoo is trying to keep people safe, even if this plan changes nothing at all."

She definitely looked happier at the thought of it all failing. I kind of understood. While it wasn't an affinity I myself possessed, Leah loved birds of all kinds. No matter how many times she was bitten, scratched, or smacked in the face by a wing, she never stopped loving them. I suspected she was another zookeeper who possessed the same animal intuition I knew I had. That was why all of the avian members of the zoo had generally thrived ever since she'd been in charge. The only exception had been when they'd all been cooped up inside and miserable, due to the threat of bird flu.

I made a point of walking past the echidna enclosure to cheer myself up. The puggles were all grown up now and most had been sent to other zoos, but a family of two adults and two babies remained and I was pleased to see them rustling through the undergrowth, as the day began to fade.

A warm hand touched my shoulder and I turned and found myself looking straight into the face of Auryn Avery, the zoo's apprentice keeper. Auryn was occasionally given a bit of a ribbing by other members of staff who, due to a case of sour grapes, thought he was being given a free ride. Auryn's father was the head of the board of directors and his grandfather owned the zoo itself. I knew it was hardly a coincidence that Auryn had got the apprenticeship, but I refused to think any less of him, or treat him any differently because of his heritage. I figured Auryn appreciated that, as we'd become friends, despite him being in his very late teens and me clinging to the second half of my twenties.

"Hey, I heard you were the one who found Ray. I'm sorry about that," he said by way of a greeting. I looked into his solemn grey eyes and reflected that despite his youth, he often displayed a maturity way beyond some of our more 'grown up' colleagues.

"It's okay. Someone had to find him," I said, rather nonsensically.

Auryn tilted his head, his light blonde, straight hair, slipping sideways over his forehead. Hours in the sun had turned him golden, like the majority of the keepers at the zoo, but he always seemed to glow. His face was fast losing the roundness of youth and his angular jaw was now covered with closely shaved stubble.

"It wasn't exactly fun finding him. He wasn't in good shape and it's not what you expect, first thing on a Saturday morning," I admitted for the first time.

Auryn nodded. "I just hope the police will find whoever it is that's responsible. My father demanded that they interview every one of the activists who've been hanging around, but he said they didn't seem keen on the idea. I think they reckon it was someone who knew him, or maybe even an accident," he said, hopefully.

I shook my head, slowly. "I know it's possible that something went wrong when he was fixing up the side of the pool and that hammer fell on him in some freak accident, but there was definitely someone else there with him." I bit my lip, not wanting to add any fuel to the already burning fires around the zoo but failing to hold the thought in. "Did the police interview the animal rights people in the end? I heard rumours of extremists coming here. People who may have a reputation for violence where animals are concerned."

Auryn sighed and looked ten years older for a second. Privileged or not, home life must be challenging when the two generations above you had total control of the zoo's future. It meant it was likely he'd been privy to all of the behind-the-scenes action that had gone on due to the investigation.

"Yeah, I think the police said they'd ask around, but how is that going to help? No one's going to say anything. I thought they'd be, you know, investigating... doing some real detective work. Not asking a few questions and hoping the killer will be thick enough to hand themselves in." He blushed, realising he'd spoken too passionately. "I mean, not that there's necessarily a killer at all, but, you know..."

I nodded. I did know. With all of the bad feeling that still dogged the zoo in the wake the poisoning accident, it did seem like a stretch to believe that Ray's death was merely a tragic coincidence.

"Hopefully they'll find something soon," I offered, feeling just as helpless as I knew Auryn did.

He shrugged. "That, or we'll just all wait around until someone else dies," he said - so bitterly it stunned me.

"You think that might happen?"

He blinked, coming out of his daze. "I don't know. I hope not! It's just... we know so little," he explained before we lapsed into silence.

"It'll all get sorted in the end and things will go back to normal," I said, but the words sounded hollow to my ears.

"I guess so. Well, I've got, you know, stuff to do, so I'll go do that."

I watched him go, wondering if there was something better that I could have said. The apprentice keeper was clearly taking the death hard, and I could understand why he was frustrated. All of us were. The animal rights activists had previously just been a thorn in our sides, but with the police classing the death as 'suspicious', they were more despised than ever.

"If they're smart, they won't stick around here for long," I murmured, as I watched Auryn walk into the bat enclosure. I could feel the tension bubbling as well as anyone. I wondered how long it would be before the elephant in the room burst free and transformed into someone taking matters into their own hands.

"Madi!" Tiff skipped towards me with a smile on her face. "Did I just see you chatting to Auryn? He looked upset. What did you do, turn him down for a date?" she teased and I blushed (as usual) before swatting her.

"Shhh Tiff. He makes me feel like I'm twice his age."

She raised an eyebrow at me. "He's changed a lot this past year. Everyone in the shop can't get over it. You can't tell me you haven't noticed the way the girls here spend most of their time trying to get him alone?"

I shrugged. I really hadn't spent that much time observing Auryn and the attention he was apparently attracting. I left the nuances of the human drama in the zoo to Tiff, who would always fill me in. Just like she was doing now.

"He doesn't seem interested in any of them though. He's polite, but he never talks long with anyone. You're the only person he seems to open up to," she said, pointedly.

"I just treat him like I'd want to be treated, if I was in his situation. He probably thinks they're trying to suck up to him because of his legacy."

Tiff tilted her head from side to side. "I'm sure some of the girls imagine there would be perks to dating him because of that, but mostly, I'm pretty sure they're more impressed by those guns he's been working on all winter." She flexed her bicep to show me.

I pulled a face. "I cannot believe you just used the word 'guns' in casual conversation."

Tiff snorted. "But, just so you know, people do notice that you guys talk a lot and not everyone knows, like I do, that you're just friends," she warned.

"You mean people really think that...?" I was completely surprised. I'd never noticed anyone watching our exchanges, but it was a fact of life that nothing was private at the zoo. I just hadn't thought anyone cared.

"People think you've got something going on, and they aren't all happy about it, either," Tiff continued.

I laughed before I could help myself. Petite, with glasses and permanently wavy hair that refused to cooperate no matter how much I begged, I was hardly the zoo babe. I wasn't unhappy with the way I looked. I liked my green eyes and the way my nose perked up at the end. Sometimes I even liked the way the pale scattering of freckles across my nose looked. That was, until the sun made them multiply beyond all reason. I was happy as pie in my own skin, but I would never have expected to become the focus of any jealousy.

"You just be careful how you go. I don't like to speak badly of anyone, but some of those girls can be pretty spiteful," Tiff said, inclining her beautiful, strawberry blonde head.

I wondered if Tiff had found herself on the receiving end of any of that spite but somehow I doubted it. Tiff attracted the attention of pretty much every male to ever walk the earth, but she was so kind and sweet, other girls always saw her as an ally, not an enemy. She'd even been voted the zoo's 'unsung hero' at this year's Christmas staff party.

I was far more used to flying under the radar.

"Hey, how's the comic coming on?" Tiff abruptly changed the conversation topic as we walked through the bat walkway and came out in the midst of visitors and other members of staff, AKA 'listening ears'.

I looked around, hoping that no one would be at all interested in what Tiff had just said. "Tiff, someone could hear," I quietly complained, but she just shrugged.

"No one will be able to make any sense of it, chill out."

"I just don't want anyone to find out that my comic even exists," I said, and then realised how dumb that sounded.

Tiff gave me a look that confirmed it. "Come on, your work is great. I'm your biggest fan and not just 'cos we're friends. You're a great artist and you know it. You told me last week that people were starting to send you emails, so you must be doing well. You have fans!"

"Well, none of them were rude at least," I mumbled, feeling faintly embarrassed by her praise. I shook myself. "It's just, we both know it's mostly fictitious, names changed and all that, but I'd be so, so dead if anyone here figured out I was writing and drawing a comic about life at the zoo."

"I'm sure you'll keep it a secret just fine. It's not as if you've got a picture of yourself on your website, right?" Tiff said.

I tried to nod convincingly, pushing away thoughts of the 'about' page on my site, which mostly consisted of a giant picture of my face. Come to think of it, I was probably wearing my uniform in the photo. I should really re-evaluate my strategy for remaining anonymous.

"How are your maps going?" I asked Tiff, and now it was her turn to be shy.

"Pretty good! I've made sales on Etsy and everything. I never thought anyone would buy them…" She trailed off, and I smiled.

Tiff designed some fantastic, fiction inspired maps of the world that the online fandoms had gone nuts for.

"Maybe one day…" She paused and we exchanged a smile.

It was a long running joke between us that maybe one day we'd both be able to quit the day job. To be honest, I wasn't sure if either of us would quit, even if our hobbies made enough for us to live off. We both loved our jobs (most of the time) and what was better than doing what you loved? Having a successful hobby was just the cherry on the cake.

"Anyway, I'd better get going and serve up dinner to the menagerie," I said with a smile and waved to Tiff as we parted ways.

My mind strayed back to what she'd said about people noticing my friendship with Auryn, but I couldn't bring myself to take it seriously. It would be super obvious to anyone who observed for more than a passing moment that we weren't anything other than friends. Still... a smile lifted my mouth for a second. It was unusual to find myself the subject of envy.

The late afternoon into evening passed without much incident. I observed that the penguin posse I was currently responsible for had started picking at the hole in the side of their pool again. It was getting larger by the day and water was slopping through it into the hollow space between the walls. I made a mental note to pass the news on to Morgan, so he could hopefully get someone out to fix it. I'd done patch-up tasks before, but I was less than enthusiastic about this one. I thought that was fair, considering that a zookeeper had died presumably trying to fix that very hole. One of the builders busy making a mess of the capybaras' new enclosure could jolly well do the job.

"Enjoy, little Pingus," I said to the small flock of Humboldt penguins, who flung themselves into the water after the fresh batch of fish I'd just lobbed in. I hesitated for a moment, staring through the water at the place where I'd seen Ray lying with his head caved in. Around me, I could hear the sounds of excited children, watching the last feed of the day and batting their hands against the underwater viewing window - despite notices specifically asking them not to.

My mind floated through all of the different conversations I'd had and I wondered if Ray's death might just be the start of things to come.

I hoped not.

"Good day, Madi?" James, the keeper in charge of rodents and small mammals strolled in to the storeroom as I was washing up the penguins' buckets.

"The usual. How was yours?" I asked, taking the opportunity to smile at the other keeper.

James was something of an enigma. He was in his twenties with neat dark hair and a face that he managed to keep pale year round - despite the amount of sun exposure we zookeepers experienced. His unusual complexion was further set off by his eyes that were so dark brown, they were nearly black. It had given rise to a few people calling him the zoo's resident vampire. While I knew that was nonsense, James was undeniably strange at times. Like the majority of the zookeepers I knew, he loved the animals he specialised in and had once told me that he'd decided to become a zookeeper because his parents had never let him have the pets he wanted as a child. He'd brought every single rat and mouse he could lay his hands on into the house. I could only imagine what his poor parents had been through.

He'd told me all of that during one of his exceedingly rare chatty moments. James liked to keep himself to himself. He had a way of gliding through the zoo without attracting any attention and he had even been called out on not attending staff meetings, when in fact he'd been standing at the back all along.

"My day was okay, thank you for asking. I heard you

found poor Ray. I hope you're doing okay," he offered and I tried to hide my surprise at his sentiment.

"I'm fine. I just wish that there didn't have to be a body to find," I said, and looked quickly at James, wondering if that had made any sense at all.

"I hear you." He ran a finger across one of his dead straight eyebrows - a gesture I found odd to do whilst thinking. "I just hope everything blows over soon. There's not a good feeling here, is there?" he said, and then slipped away out of the door without waiting for a response.

I stood there thinking about his cryptic words for a moment before shaking them off. As I'd said, James was an enigma.

Even though it was clocking out time, I decided to take a stroll down to the cat barn. I'd managed to feed them earlier in the day, but hadn't seen any sign of the pregnant cat. This time, I did my best to creep around the corner and even saw two of the younger cats scrapping playfully on the dusty floor, but there was still no sign of the black cat with the white socks. I shrugged it off. Feral cats liked to move around. She might have managed to haul herself off on a hunting trip, or perhaps she'd just decided that the barn wasn't the place to have her kittens after all. Only time would tell. For now, I'd just have to keep an eye out for her.

I walked back through the food storage warehouse and into the 'backstage area' of the zoo. The sun was dipping in the sky, bathing the zoo in a beautiful pinky orange light. I smiled and decided to walk back to the entrance the visitors' way. It always soothed me to see the animals begin their nightly routines - whether that meant waking up, or going to sleep.

I'd just passed the meerkats when I heard footsteps. Technically, everyone should be on their way home by now, but there were occasionally a few of us who stayed later to finish up little tasks. Maybe it was a reaction to knowing what had befallen Ray when he'd stayed back after hours, but I pressed myself flat against the wooden poles that ran up the side of the meerkats' enclosure. The footsteps came closer. I briefly wondered how foolish I'd feel if someone caught me acting so strangely, but the steps passed by. The walker was being careful, but the heavy work boots he was wearing did nothing to muffle his steps. I found myself looking at the back view of a well-muscled man with a tribal tattoo peeking from beneath his sleeve. It was Lowell, the new builder I'd asked about earlier that day.

As soon as he rounded the corner, I discovered I'd been holding my breath. I let it out and breathed normally for a couple of seconds, wondering if what I'd just seen was in any way significant. Sure, people stayed late at the zoo, but not usually builders. They were brought in for a limited number of hours a day - unless the work was especially pressing - and they would be paid overtime to stay. But matters that were deemed 'pressing' were only ever emergencies, where there was a good chance the zoo could get sued, or reported to health and safety authorities if the problem wasn't fixed quickly. There were no current projects that fit that bill.

I realised I couldn't think of a single good reason why Lowell might be creeping around the zoo after hours - which in my mind left only bad ones.

3

POINTING FINGERS

My pencil skated across the page as I sketched out an expansion on one of my storyboards. I reflected that it was lucky I had so much material drawn out in rough to use, as finding that 'funny' inspiration wasn't likely to happen this week. I frowned and focused on the knitted brows of the pompous zoo manager, who liked to boss everyone around, before his schemes would humorously fall apart and result in slapstick disaster for him. The character of Mr Masters, the manager, wasn't based on anyone in particular. It was more an amalgamation of anyone who'd annoyed me that week. This was my petty writer's revenge.

I paused for a moment to open my email inbox and look at the five new messages I'd received, all with my comic's title as the subject of the message. I could already see from the email previews that none of them were rude, negative, or angry. On the contrary, it sounded like they liked my work. I was fully intending on replying to all of the emails, just as soon as I'd got over the initial excitement that people were actually writing to me. Those five emails were just today's offering. Yesterday I'd had four messages, and the day before that, six!

I clicked to my webcomic's dashboard and looked at the stats, noting that the number of visitors was steadily increasing. Ever since I'd done a little research into what it took to start your own online comic and how to get readership, I'd seen people saying that you started slowly and then once you got a few readers, you'd soon find your readership double and then quadruple as word spread like a virus.

Starting the comic was the hardest part. I'd done it for the love of it, just because I enjoyed making up the story lines and drawing them. When I'd been featured on a webcomic site and a few people had visited, that had been great. Now things were starting to take on a life of their own. I'd even seen one of my panels shared on a Facebook page, dedicated to people who took care of animals.

That had been when I'd started to worry about what would happen if anyone at the zoo found the comic. I hastily clicked to the 'about me' page and deleted the unwise photo of myself.

There.

My secret was hopefully safe, although the little voice in my head reminded me that nothing truly disappeared once it had been posted on the internet. My photo could already have been shared far and wide without my knowledge. I might currently be the face of any number of 'Russian wives' advertisements, although I sincerely doubted it. It was far more likely that any pirated picture of me would be used for a campaign that featured 'before' and 'after' photos. Unless it was an advert for the results of eating too much chocolate, my photo would not be the 'after' image.

I opened the first email and realised it was yet another request for prints of the comic to be sold. I nudged my glasses back up my nose and made a mental note to ask Tiff all about Etsy. Perhaps I could open up a store and see how it went.

My gaze drifted down to rest on the page in front of me where the squirrel monkeys were in the process of escaping again. I smiled darkly at their deceptively adorable faces. Few people realised they were probably the most vicious animals at the zoo. This time, in the comic world of *Monday's Menagerie*, the squirrel monkeys had found a child's plastic spade and were currently digging their way beneath the zoo in another doomed bid for freedom. While I would be surprised if Avery Zoo's squirrel monkeys managed to use a child's spade to dig their way out, I wouldn't put the idea of digging to freedom beyond them. They were as devious as animals came and seemed to escape with regularity. Even so, Tom, the keeper in charge of primates, still refused to try any of the changes I'd suggested making to their enclosure. I sighed, thinking back to the equally frustrating encounter I'd had with him earlier in the day. With some people, you always knew you were fighting a losing battle. But it had never put me off trying.

I clicked on PhotoShop and put the final touches to a comic I'd half coloured in. I tilted my head, giving it one last check for spelling and grammar, before I saved it as a png and uploaded it to the comic. I had a brief moment of satisfaction when I pressed 'post' and decided to reward my small achievement with an evening hot chocolate. Living alone as I did, no one else was going to celebrate it, so it was down to me to highlight these moments.

Sometimes I wondered what it would be like to have a boyfriend who lived with me. I'd had longish term relationships before, but that had been years ago and none of them had felt right enough to move to that next stage of living together. That was probably why they'd all fallen apart.

I'd thought about getting a pet. My mother had long

wanted a grandchild, and as an only child, all of her hopes rested on me. For now, I knew she'd be lucky to have a grand-cat or a grand-dog, with my lack of boyfriend finding abilities.

I stirred my hot chocolate, watching the darker threads of chocolate mingle with the milk. Did I want a boyfriend right now? I thought about it and decided I probably didn't. Things were infinitely simpler without another person to consider and it wasn't as if anything in my working life was simple. I had more than enough to occupy myself.

I reassured myself that this was of course the only reason I wasn't already married with two and a half kids.

I smiled and walked up to my bedroom with the hot chocolate. I'd decided to spend the rest of the evening chilling out with whatever fantasy book I could lay my hands on. Perhaps I'd start *The Hobbit* again and travel that world, or maybe I'd choose one of my guilty pleasures - post-apoca-lyptic adventures. I knew some people thought they were silly, but I loved the edge-of-your seat action, when the protagonist ran from the giant horde of zombies. I also figured the more I read, the more likely my zombie action plan would be completely foolproof, when the time came.

I selected a book and slid beneath the covers, switching my mind off from all of the happenings of the day.

The entrance to the zoo was full of people the next morning. As there was still half an hour to go before the zoo opened, it was definitely unusual.

I got out of my car and made my way towards the throng. My heart jolted. I wondered if someone else had been found dead. I quashed the thought and decided to find out the answer before jumping to conclusions. It wasn't long before angry voices reached my ears and I assigned the loudest voice to Colin, the zookeeper who took care of the equine and hoofed animals at the zoo.

It didn't take a genius to figure out what had made him so angry.

Colin's car - a rather ancient, black Mercedes parked right outside the zoo - had been vandalised. Someone had taken a can of red spray paint and written 'Murder Farmer' on the bonnet of his car. There was another bright red slogan across the side doors that sneered 'Cattle Killer'. I looked at the words and a memory from long ago resurfaced.

"I was here all night looking after Louisa and her calf and this is what I get when I come out here in the morning to drive home for some sleep! We all know exactly who did this. Now I want to know why the hell no one is doing anything to stop them?" Colin was shouting at the top of his voice with his finger outstretched towards the small group of people, who'd already started to drift in and hang around the gates. A few of the animal rights activists raised their placards and cheered when they heard Colin shouting, which hardly helped their case.

I caught Morgan rolling his eyes, although I wasn't sure if it was at Colin, or the group of animal annoyances. I still failed to see how marching around outside a zoo helped save animals.

A police car swung into the car park and a couple of officers got out. I vaguely recognised them from the penguin pool crime scene. They greeted Colin and began asking him the usual questions. He loudly berated the lack of CCTV in the car park, threatening to personally install his own in future. Then he flung accusations around but the protesters either didn't hear, or ignored him now that the police were there. The fun was over. The group of people who'd gathered by the car sensed it, too, as they began to dissipate and walk away.

I stayed for a few moments more, looking at the writing on the car. A past incident, which had occurred the last time the zoo had attracted more than their fair share of protesters, rose in my mind.

Danny Emeridge had been the last apprentice zookeeper that the zoo had taken on, before Auryn had decided that his future lay with the family business. He was the sort of guy that no one had a bad word to say about and despite his apprentice status, he'd worked as hard as any keeper.

That was before it had happened.

He'd been walking across the car park when they struck. Danny had stayed late, so no one was around to see. I'd found him an hour or so later and had called an ambulance and the police. They'd saved his life, but he'd never returned to the zoo.

The people who had done it to him went unpunished. It was another open case that everyone knew would never be solved. There had been rumours though, a lot of rumours. The animal activists had finally taken a step too far - they'd attacked one of us. People at the zoo had demanded justice, but the activists had closed ranks and allegedly nothing further could be done. The case had been dropped and eventually the protesters had drifted away, leaving the zoo in peace... until now. I wondered if the police had bothered to look into that past case and note the similar circumstances that tied together Danny's attack and Ray's potential murder. I thought about bringing it up with them, but found I simply didn't want to get involved. It was time for the police to do their own detective work and if I could avoid being dragged through those past memories again, that would be a big plus.

After a dramatic start to the day, the morning turned out to be a quiet one. It was Tuesday and for some reason the general public had chosen to be elsewhere. A few families on their summer holidays milled around, but it was nice to have a day's rest from the usual summer holiday bedlam. I always counted down the days until school started again.

I wasn't a children hater. I thought children were great. It was more their parents that I had a problem with, or more specifically, a particular sort of parent. When you saw parents drop their kids over fences, or when kids banged on the glass of enclosures and ran wild, generally making the experience unpleasant for other families, I always bore witness to the kind of adult I didn't like. They were usually busy chatting to their other half, or oblivious on their phone while all of this was going on.

I blinked away the negative thoughts and tried to go back to appreciating the relative quiet of the zoo. I'd just finished tidying up the fennec foxes' enclosure when I saw Tiff waving at me through the glass.

"Hey," I said, when I'd walked back around. I suddenly noticed she wasn't alone. A girl wearing the pale green shirt that marked zoo volunteers and temporary staff was stood next to her. She had brown, shoulder length hair, that swung in a straight sheet and dark brown eyes. There wasn't a scrap of makeup on her face and there was a definite tomboy air about her. This was a person who I suspected didn't give a damn about what anyone had to say about the way she looked.

"Madi, this is Alison Rowley. She's going to be helping out in the shop and everywhere else this summer," Tiff said with a smile.

I extended my hand and the other girl shook it with a shy smile. We made eye contact and I immediately got the sense that this was someone I would get on with. "It's nice to meet you. So you're a summer odd job worker?"

She nodded. "That's me! I need to get some cash together.

Trips to Thailand don't fund themselves," she said, raising her dark eyebrows.

"How are the fennecs doing? I'm guessing they're up to see what's going on in their enclosure, given that they're usually nocturnal."

"They are rather curious," I admitted, looking back at the three pairs of giant ears that could be seen poking out behind an artificial dune I'd just re-dug.

"Are those the mated pair?" Alison asked and I nodded. The third, smaller fox hopped along behind them. "That must be a pup, but he looks pretty old. How come you decided to let him stay? I know in the wild they sometimes stay together, but couldn't it bring problems in a zoo?"

"We're seeing how it goes, actually. As they're a mated pair, he's not exactly a threat and no other zoo wants to involve him in their breeding programme, due to a little defect you might have noticed. See the way he hops along? It's because he was born with one leg significantly shorter than the other three," I explained.

I tilted my head at Alison, taking in her rather tatty jeans with the rainbow ribbon pinned to a safety pin adorning the side seam. She may only be doing odd jobs, but she'd need to be careful or she'd have one of the managers on at her case about dress code.

"You're a fan of fennec foxes then?" I asked and to my surprise her cheeks turned pink.

"Yeah, I just like animals, I guess," she said with a shrug and turned back to Tiff, who'd been busy texting whilst we'd had the conversation.

"Oh, yeah I guess our break is over. Nice seeing you Madi!" Tiff said, whisking Alison away with her. I watched them go with slightly narrowed eyes. I found myself wanting to like Alison, which was probably why Tiff had bothered to introduce us in the first place, but there was also something a little off about her. If she had that much animal knowledge bursting out at the seams, why was she content to just take a summer 'odd job' role? Her claim that she was saving for a trip to Thailand also seemed a little fishy. Perhaps I was stereotyping, but she didn't behave like your average adventure seeking 'Instagram girl', who thought Thailand was *the* exotic location to be.

I shook my head. Perhaps I was just being paranoid, but Alison's in depth knowledge of animals did make me wonder. I frowned as I walked to do my next job. I hoped the zoo's screening policy was up to scratch. Of one thing I was sure, I was going to keep a close eye on Alison Rowley.

"Madi! How's it going?"

I turned to see Tom climb out of the squirrel monkeys' enclosure.

"Good, thanks," I said, mystified as to why he was speaking to me. The only words Tom and I usually exchanged were words of disagreement.

"I never got a chance to say when I saw you the other day, tough break finding Ray." He pulled what I assumed was his attempt at a sympathetic expression. It wasn't pretty.

One hand went to his thick thatch of sandy hair and he ruffled it unconsciously. I waited for him to speak, figuring there must be some favour he needed.

"Hey, uh, you're looking good at the moment, Madi. I was wondering if you fancied going and getting dinner sometime?" he asked, his blue eyes deadly serious.

I made a small choking noise and did my best to stamp on the urge to laugh.

What on earth was he thinking? We'd spent the last two years arguing over the various changes and additions to the zoo and now he wanted to take me out on a date?

I suddenly realised that Tom was still staring at me,

waiting for a response. "It was nice of you to ask, but no thank you," I said, hoping that would be the end of it.

"Oh, you already got someone else in your life then? No one from the zoo, right?" he said, and I fought the urge to roll my eyes. I hated men who assumed that when you turned them down it couldn't possibly be because you weren't interested in them. It had to be because some other guy had got there first.

"No, I just don't want to go for dinner." I kept my voice as light as I could. "By the way, you might want to trim that clematis. It's getting pretty close to the squirrel monkey enclosure." I nodded to the twisting tendrils of plant that were escaping the trellis on the side of the bridge that ran across the wide stretch of water which marked the squirrel monkeys' enclosure boundary on the west side. The plant had started to creep across the wood panelling towards the monkeys.

"Looks okay to me," he said with a shrug and threw me a final unreadable look before striding away.

Now I really did roll my eyes. That was Tom through and through - he'd never take any advice you tried to give him.

I thought about that look he'd given me and figured it was disbelief, plain and simple. He couldn't believe that someone like me had dared to turn someone like him down.

I snorted. "Proves it was the right decision," I said to myself, but I hadn't even been tempted. The most mystifying thing was why he'd even thought to ask in the first place. I'd assumed we had a respectful mutual deep dislike thing going on. I shrugged it off and decided to get back to work.

The next stop was the still-miserable capybaras. I'd filled some rubber toys with treats. The balls needed to pushed around to get the treats to fall out and I was hoping it might distract them from their less than salubrious surroundings - at least for an hour or so.

I'd just finished giving a talk to the public about the zoo's echidnas when I saw the new builder, Lowell, walk by. Having finished up, I thanked my audience and walked off in the direction he'd been going. It wasn't long before I had to conclude I'd lost him and I wondered why I'd even considered following him in the first place. It was day time and he was supposed to be working. What reason did I have to suspect he was up to something?

I shrugged off my worries and pushed open the gate between the giant anteater enclosure and the wallabies, that led to the intricate behind-the-scenes passages used by zoo staff. I was on my way to the food store when I heard male voices, deep in conversation. They were from the back entrance of the bat exhibit.

I took a step towards the door and hesitated, realising I didn't have a good reason to be going that way, as I'd only fed the bats half an hour ago. Unfortunately, it was at that moment the door swung open and Lowell stepped out.

We stared at each other in surprise.

"You startled me. I was just popping in to check that Binky had her dinner. She hasn't been eating for a couple of days," I invented, quickly realising I was over-explaining. The man in front of me just kept on looking with his intense, dark eyes.

Then, to my surprise, Mr Avery Senior walked through the door after Lowell. I tried not to change my facial expression as I realised it had been these two men I'd heard talking just now. I wished I'd been able to catch the words, but all I'd heard were two voices speaking in the serious undertone you used when you didn't want anyone to overhear you.

"Mr Avery, Sir, it's very nice to see you," I said, giving the owner of the zoo his due respect. The old man nodded back and said hello in a vacant way that proved he had absolutely no clue who I was. Then he walked away, leaving me alone with Lowell.

We looked at each other for another long beat before turning and walking off in opposite directions.

My mind was racing as I went through the motions of the tasks I had planned for the remainder of the day. What was a rookie builder doing talking with the owner of the zoo? Perhaps I could have justified it if it were Rich, the leader of the gang, but Lowell was the new guy. I couldn't think of any business he might have with Mr Avery Senior. Come to think of it, I wasn't too sure what business Mr Avery himself had being at the zoo. He was still the registered owner, but he'd handed the control of the day-to-day running over to his son, Erin Avery, a long time ago. Erin now sat as the head of the board of directors.

I struggled to piece together a logical reason for the two unlikely men to be together and I could only think of something that would surely raise an eyebrow or two, if it ever got out.

My mind replayed the intense look that Lowell had given me and I found, to my surprise, that I wasn't sure if I wanted to believe what the facts appeared to suggest.

4

CAT BURGLARS

The posters appeared just in time for the weekend.

I had felt like I was holding my breath all through the week after what had happened to Colin's car, but absolutely nothing had happened. When I'd walked past the group of protesters, I'd even noticed that their number had diminished.

As it turned out, that was probably because half of them were busy putting together their next dirty trick.

I saw my first poster when I exited the giant anteater enclosure. A piece of blue, A4 paper was being blown about by the breeze and landed facedown on the floor in front of me. I picked it up and read the headline.

CONDEMN the Avery animal MURDERERS!

I skimmed my eyes over the obviously hastily prepared poster. It cited the recent death of the serval, the zoo's employing of one Colin Campbell, a known villain of the dairy industry, and…

My eyebrows rose in disbelief. They were claiming that Ray Myers' death in the penguin pool was a clear sign that the zoo was abusing animals, as his incompetence must have got him killed.

Well! I was about to crumple the nasty piece of paper up when I read the call to action at the bottom of the page. It was pushing for all zoo workers to turn their managers in and reveal the dark truth of what was really going on at Avery Zoo. I frowned. That was a little more interesting. I'd assumed that this poster was intended to shock the general public but it was infinitely sneakier than that. They were trying to pull us apart from the inside by making everyone question who could be trusted.

I closed my eyes and realised their plan might actually succeed. The volunteers were already furious about the managements' handling of their private social media conversations. It wouldn't take much to drive a wedge in when one was already in place.

I crumpled the paper into a ball and pushed it into the nearest bin. A flash of blue caught my eye and I spied another poster taped to the meerkats' enclosure. I tore it down but my eyes were attuned to the colour now and I began seeing them everywhere. The protestors must have found someone to pretend to be a visitor and then plaster the zoo with posters. They'd done it just after opening time, while half the staff were admittedly, still waking up.

I shook my head and wondered if there would be repercussions for this. There was CCTV within the zoo, although it didn't cover every space, otherwise the police would know the identity of whoever was helping Ray in the penguin enclosure. I frowned as I suddenly realised it probably wasn't just by chance that they'd known where the blind spots were, but the more I thought about it, the more likely it seemed to me that it was someone he knew who had done it. They'd had to get close enough to him to either drop, or swing the sledgehammer - depending whether you subscribed to the 'accidental death but too scared to admit to it' theory, or murder. They'd also known where the light switches were to turn the lights off when they left and they'd done so out of habit. So where did that leave the theory about the animal rights peoples' involvement? Perhaps Ray's death was completely unrelated.

I shook my head again and started pulling down the posters, feeling sorry for both Colin and Ray Myers' memory. All Colin was guilty of, was working in the dairy industry and daring to prosecute a group of activists who had broken into his farm with the misguided intention of freeing the cows. They'd let them loose and they'd promptly run onto a motorway, killing both cows and motorists. It was a terrible tragedy which had resulted in lengthy prosecutions for the perpetrators. It had somehow turned Colin into animal rights public enemy number one, for daring to seek justice.

People were going to be very angry when they found these posters. Tensions were already running high at the zoo, with wild theories flying around about how far the activists were willing to go for their cause. The police had so far failed to share any progress on Ray's case and I suspected it would be the same story with this new incident. The animal rights group would have found a stranger and paid them to do their dirty work. Their face on CCTV would mean nothing and the group would gleefully deny any involvement.

I crumpled up my tenth poster and binned it, nodding to members of the shop team who I saw doing the same. A death, a vandalised car, and now these hate posters... something was bubbling away at the zoo and I didn't think it would be long before the pot spilled over.

Beams of late afternoon sunshine sliced through gaps between wooden slats, illuminating thousands of tiny dust particles in the barn. I stopped poking my head around the corner and risked a silent step forwards. At least… it had seemed silent to me. There was the usual flurry of activity as the feral cats retreated behind their bales.

"Come on, it's not as if I'm the one who is responsible for making sure you get fed and survive! Oh. Wait." I muttered as I rounded the corner carrying a fresh bowl of cat food.

Not all of the cats had fled. That was because one of them wasn't able to do much running at the minute.

"My, my, you are pregnant!" I said, placing the bowl down and dashing over to the rotund black cat. It did its best to slink away at top speed, but top speed wasn't much at the moment, so I was able to untie the sweater from my waist and nab her.

Once four of the five pointy ends were safely encased in the sweater (which I very much doubted would ever be the same again) I gently felt her tummy and noted the movement within. I was no vet by any means, but I thought I felt four separate moving lumps. While I did this, the black cat actually settled down and sat still, albeit in a sulk. I risked a stroke of the head and was tolerated. A second later I heard a purr.

The cat and I stared at one another.

"How embarrassing for you," I said, releasing the cat's legs from captivity and letting her slink off into the shadows again. I wasn't fooled. Much as this cat coveted the feral lifestyle, I suspected I actually had a disgruntled ex-pet on my hands.

"Well, I won't take you back, but I'll keep checking to make sure you and the kids are doing okay," I said, figuring she would probably give birth in the next 48 hours. Again, I was no vet, but she looked really fat. I sucked my cheeks in and reflected that judgements like this one were the reason why I was never invited to baby showers.

I was smiling when I walked back out into the sunshine. I strolled along the slim pathway I'd worn in the grass from my regular trips to visit the cats, attention fixed on the blue sky and not the gaggle of sheds and outbuildings that stood opposite the entrance to the main storage warehouse.

That was why I didn't see who grabbed me.

I was yanked backwards into the dark interior of one of the sheds. The door swung shut and I struggled against the vice-like grip on my shoulders. I blindly swung an elbow behind me and was rewarded with a grunt of pain as I made contact with... well, I wan't sure, but I hoped it was something vital. The grip loosened for a second and I lurched forwards, only for my attacker to follow the movement. I ended up facedown on the floor with their full weight pressing down on top of me.

"Stop fighting me or you're going to get us both killed," a man's voice hissed. I recognised it, but what I was more familiar with was the smell of sage and sea salt that I'd noticed followed in Lowell's wake.

"What are you talking about? And what the hell are you doing here on a Saturday?" I hissed back, erring on the side of caution with a whisper.

He covered my mouth with a hand but before I could bite him to show him just how much I appreciated *that*, we both heard the sound of breaking glass. The light from beneath the door illuminated his dark eyes and I inclined my head to let him know he could let go.

We both wriggled on our stomachs, until our heads were right next to the wooden door. It had a gap of two inches or so between the slats and the dirt floor. I ignored the pain coming from several points of my body, caused by the struggle. Instead, I focused on what I could see through the narrow gap.

Two men wearing balaclavas over their otherwise innocuous jeans and long-sleeved black tops were looking around them - probably waiting to see if anyone was coming to check out the noise. I tried not to groan in frustration, knowing that while this was an area with a CCTV camera pointing directly at the door, the men's disguises demonstrated they had known it would be. I wondered if they also somehow knew that none of the zoo's cameras had a live feed. They were only there for insurance purposes, in case footage needed checking after an event had occurred.

They must have walked across the fields. That's the only way no one would have spotted them, I thought.

I watched as one of the men reached a hand through the shattered side window and stretched. He was struggling to reach the deadbolt inside that kept the door shut. The other guy held a plastic bag full of... something. It looked like white powder.

"What is that?" I whispered to Lowell, figuring the men were pretty well occupied right now.

"I'm not sure, but I think they're going to try and poison the food. I've heard about it happening before, although it's pretty extreme tactics," he said.

"Killing animals in order to make the zoo look like they're responsible for killing animals, so you can close the zoo down and save the animals. Well, that just makes perfect sense," I muttered.

Lowell quickly raised a finger to his lips and I realised I was probably speaking too loudly. We both paused and checked on the men, who were still failing to get at the deadbolt through the small window.

"Why do they even think it would work? It's going to be obvious to anyone that there's been a break-in and that the food supply may have been contaminated. It doesn't make sense," I whispered and suddenly felt super self-conscious about just how close I was lying to Lowell. He'd been on top of me just moments earlier and we were currently pressed tightly together on the floor. I felt the heat rise to my cheeks and thanked my lucky stars that it was pretty dark inside the shed.

"They're hoping it'll take people a while to notice the window and a break-in in the middle of the day is less likely to be looked for. All it would take is one keeper to need some extra supplies and not see the broken glass" Lowell whispered back.

I half-shrugged my shoulders, which turned out to be a difficult feat in such a confined space. It could be that, but it still seemed like a big chance to take after taking the risk of breaking in. So far, the group hadn't been caught committing crime, so why risk it all now with a long-shot?

All of a sudden, I saw red. It didn't matter that their plan was doomed to failure because Lowell and I had witnessed it all firsthand. What mattered was that any second now, they were going to get that deadbolt slid open and put their plan into action. I couldn't stomach the thought that there was even a chance of any animal in the zoo being subjected to their murderous tactics.

"I'm going to try and sneak around the other side. If I can make it by without being seen, I'll be able to go round and enter the warehouse from the other side. Hopefully I can surprise them and they'll run." I pushed up from the floor while Lowell turned on his side and stared at me as though I'd sprouted an extra head.

"Are you crazy?! If they see you, they'll probably kill you. Look at the evidence. You heard the rumours about extremists coming here? It looks like they've arrived and they've done a hell of a lot worse than poisoning food before," he said.

I opened my mouth to ask him why he would know so much about these so called animal rights activists but at that moment, one of the men grunted in triumph as the deadbolt slid across. I watched through a knot in the shed door as they both entered the building, pulling the door closed behind them.

It was now or never.

I pushed the shed door open and slid out before sprinting across the sunlit grass on my way around the front of the zoo - the quickest route back round to the food store. I didn't wait to see if I had been spotted or followed, but there was no shouts or sounds. Just the long, yellow grass whipping across my legs as I ran.

"Call the police, there's a break-in happening right now," I shouted as I tore through reception, wishing that someone would take me seriously. Hopefully the fact that I was flat out sprinting would be enough. It was a rare sight to say the least.

I raced through the zoo, pleased for once that I was small. People probably mistook me for a child and moved aside far more considerately than they would have for a regular-sized adult. It also meant I fitted through the small gaps between visitors who were content to move at a snail's pace.

It seemed an eternity before I reached the entrance to the food store. I stopped running and wiped my sweaty hands on my trousers, wondering if they were still inside the warehouse... wondering if this was the worst idea I'd ever had in my life. I pulled my mobile phone from my pocket and pretended to be speaking to a friend on the other end of the line. My mind, which was currently working in overdrive, supplied that it would be good pretend insurance to put off an attack, while not cluing up the men inside the warehouse that I was onto them. If I didn't hear them leaving after I entered, I'd simply go back out the same door and wait for the police to arrive. Now wasn't a good time for heroic stunts. Actually, there was never a good time for heroic stunts when you were my size.

I pushed the door open and pressed the phone to my ear, taking a breath before I began my pretend conversation. Here went nothing. I pushed the door to the food prep area open.

"Hey, Tiff, how's it going?" I paused for a second, listening as I waited by the counter.

Nothing.

That probably meant the intruders were listening, too. "Yeah, I'm not so bad. I'm doing food prep at the moment, but..." I heard a door slam shut and felt my heart jump a little, before settling down. Had they really left, or was it a ruse?

I lowered the phone, no longer pretending, and made my way cautiously to the door that separated the main food prep area from the large warehouse. I looked through the window. In the dim light, I couldn't see a sign of anyone moving and the main door was definitely shut. Had they gone, or were they still hiding in the room? I rested my palm against the dividing door before I made a decision and pushed it open.

My head snapped from side to side as I checked to see if anyone was pressed to the wall by the door, waiting to attack. There was no one in sight, not even when I scanned the warehouse. It was possible that someone was crouched down below the big food bins, but the hairs weren't standing up on the back of my neck anymore. It felt as though they'd really gone when I'd heard the door slam.

With any luck, the police would be on their way by now and the lengthy checking of all the food supplies for contamination could begin. I wouldn't want to be the person saddled with overseeing that job.

I turned my back on the empty room with a shrug and pushed on the door that led back through to the prep room, only to meet resistance. I raised my head and saw Tom looking back through the small window at me.

"Sorry, I didn't see you there!" he said, standing back from the door to allow me through.

"You're not on your way into the warehouse, are you?" I asked, feeling stupid for asking an obvious question, but not knowing another way to bring it up.

"Yeah, we're running low on several dried foods," he said, moving to sidestep me.

"You can't," I said, firmly, blocking his way and then feeling silly all over again when he looked at me in surprise. "I just saw two men break-in, and they were carrying a bag of some kind of powder. I'm not sure what they were planning, but it's possible that they might have been trying to poison the food."

His face paled. "Why would anyone do that? Do you think it's something to do with animal rights again?"

I half-nodded. "Well, they do seem to hate the zoo. You must have heard the rumours of extremists coming here. Perhaps this is one of their more extreme measures."

"Killing animals?" Tom said, raising an incredulous eyebrow. He was taking the same view that I had... until I'd seen it happen with my own eyes.

"Who knows? The police are on their way though, so we should probably just wait here until then," I said, as firmly as

I dared. I looked up at Tom and noticed his face hadn't regained any of its colour

"I just… can't believe anyone would do that." He thrust his hands deep into his work jeans pockets.

I merely nodded in reply. There was nothing further to say, so we just stood there in silence until the police arrived.

Perhaps it was because they'd been getting a lot of practice recently, but the investigation didn't take as long as I'd feared. The warehouse was cordoned off and large samples were taken from every one of the food containers, with the reassurances that even the tiniest amount of contaminant would show up. The zoo could do without having to bin what was probably thousands of pounds worth of food, but they also wanted assurances that the animals would all be safe.

With such a worrying potential threat, it wasn't long before Erin Avery, the head of the board of directors, showed up. More surprising was the appearance of Mr Avery Senior, the zoo owner. Perhaps the recent troubles had inspired him to re-engage with the zoo's affairs.

It wasn't long before the police got round to interviewing me and I found myself with a dilemma. Did I admit that I hadn't been the only witness to see the break-in? My gaze swung across the room and met with Mr Avery Senior's watery blue eyes. He shook his head once from left to right. I immediately dropped my eyes and focussed on the question the police officer had just asked.

So, Mr Avery didn't want Lowell's involvement to be known, at least, that was what I assumed the signal had implied. I wondered why.

I frowned and said a few more words about how it was that I'd been in the right place to witness the break-in. I told them about the cats in the barn.

Fortunately, the police never asked if I was alone or not

when I'd seen the intruders, so I didn't have to lie. I guess they assumed I must have been on my own, as any honest person would have no reason to cover for someone else. I bit my tongue. I liked to think of myself as an honest person, but the lines were definitely blurring right now.

The police officer had just finished up his questioning when Detective Rob Treesden himself walked over. My belly did a flip, as I wildly entertained ideas that the detective already knew I'd not told the truth and was coming over to arrest me. Or worse - what if this little mis-truth had led to them suspecting I was responsible for the death of Ray? I slammed a lid down on all those wild thoughts and summoned up what I hoped passed for a smile.

He frowned at me, which probably meant it wasn't one of my best. Or perhaps he just didn't like smiling. "Whilst inves-tigating the recent incidents that have occurred at the zoo, your name came up in connection with something that happened in the past." My stomach flipped again before I figured out what he must be referring to.

"Do you mean what happened to Danny Emeridge?" I cautiously asked, and the detective nodded. I tried not to breath a visible sigh of relief over avoiding being tripped up. Not that I was a criminal by any stretch of the imagination, but talking to the police always made me feel guilty of something.

"If you could tell us everything you remember from the night you found Danny," the detective prompted.

I nodded, thinking back to something I would rather forget. "Everything I saw, I put in the statement I gave then," I said, but he made a 'go on' gesture with his hand.

This time I didn't hide my sigh. "Well, I'd stayed late, although I forget the reason why. I was walking across the car park to where my car was parked, and I passed the picnic barn and saw something out of the corner of my eye. I guess because I spend all day looking after animals, the movement attracted my attention, but as soon as I took a few steps closer, I realised it was a person, huddled in a ball on the ground. I realised it was Danny, the apprentice keeper at the zoo back then. I saw blood on the gravel and while he wouldn't show me his face, I could tell he was hurt pretty badly. I pulled out my phone and called the ambulance. I remember looking around, but there was no one in sight and no sign of anyone. I'd done first aid training and they always say that when people are badly injured, you should try and keep them talking, so I did what I could. Danny didn't want to talk, but I kept talking to him. I never managed to get a word back and every time I'd try and get a look at whatever had happened, he'd just pull away. Eventually, the ambulance and police arrived and I told them what I've just told you. I'm guessing you know they never caught the people who did it," I finished.

The detective nodded, not bothering to write anything down, which didn't surprise me. I hadn't been lying when I'd said I'd already told them everything I remembered from that night.

"Who do you think was responsible?" he asked me.

I looked at him in surprise. His aquamarine eyes regarded me seriously.

"No evidence was ever found but... there were a lot of animal rights people protesting at the zoo back then. Danny would have made a convenient target. He was wearing the zoo's uniform and walking on his own. I thought it was probably a few crazy members of the group who did it then and I think it probably is again now," I said, quietly.

The detective inclined his head. "Thank you," he said, dismissing me, before walking away to confer with the other officers.

I stood in the warehouse for a few moments longer,

looking at the broken window and wondering what would have happened if they had managed to execute their plan without anyone bearing witness. I considered what might have befallen me if Lowell hadn't dragged me into that shed. Most of all, I wondered what Lowell was really doing at the zoo because I was damn sure that he wasn't just a builder.

5

THE GREAT ESCAPE

Monday was rather wetter than I'd been expecting. The source of the water was not the weather, which remained uncharacteristically good for British summertime. It was the fault of Olive the otter, who had decided that she definitely didn't want to be caught by me or anyone else. I'd drafted Leah in to help me, but as the otters were my responsibility (ever since Ray had died) she'd spent more time laughing at my efforts than actually helping.

"Leah!" I yelled, as I slipped on the slick stones and sat down in the stream. Olive eluded my net again, but ran straight to the other keeper, who neatly scooped her up. I tried not to scowl when I clambered out of the stream with the sounds of visitors' laughter following me.

"We got her, yay!" Leah said, raising the net a little and grinning. I rolled my eyes but couldn't help smiling back. I knew I looked ridiculous. Now I'd have to squelch my way back to the staffroom and see if there were any trousers I could borrow for the rest of the day - no doubt with the legs rolled up a lot.

"If she's just been eating too much after all this effort, I'll be pretty ticked off," I admitted to Leah, who just kept smiling.

The reason we'd had to catch Olive the otter was because I'd noticed her putting on a bit of weight and exhibiting a few other signs as well. As Olive was a relatively young otter, and quite a new addition to the zoo, this could be her first potential litter, so I'd decided a trip to the vet for a checkup would be wise. If it turned out she wasn't pregnant after all, the vet would probably have a thing or two to say about diet.

I made eye contact with the otter, whom Leah had just transferred to a travel carrier. She looked back at me with resentment in her beady eyes before squawking. I felt my mouth twist and Leah started giggling again.

"Right, I'm going to get her to the vet before she causes any more comedy at my expense," I said, already feeling tired despite the day only just beginning. I thanked Leah, a little dubiously, for her help and she assured me she'd be willing to do it again any time - any time at all.

I walked through the maze of paths behind the exhibits. It wasn't long before I arrived at the staffroom with an irate otter making her presence known in the carrier by my side. I rested her on a table in the middle of the room and she settled down as soon as she lost sight of me, presumably to sulk.

I shook my head and wondered if Ray had put up with the same kind of behaviour. I looked back over at the travel carrier and wondered if perhaps over time, Olive and I could become friends. I knew it probably wouldn't happen. There was a zookeeper position open at the zoo and I was hoping that the directors would attempt to fill it soon. Things might feel more normal then.

After delving around in the lost property box, I came up with a pair of jeans that would do and popped off to the loo to change. While I was changing I thought some more about that job opening and couldn't help wondering if the board were deliberately delaying their decision to see if we could get by without an extra keeper. It wouldn't surprise me if they saw it as an opportunity to cut the budget. It seemed to me that they were focussing on bringing in large, flashy, amusement park style attractions. It felt like the animals were being pushed into second place.

Clad in my poorly fitting 'new' jeans I walked back into the staffroom to pick up Olive but found my eye drawn to a bright, orange bit of paper that had been pinned to the noticeboard. An emergency meeting of the board of directors had been called and the meeting title was listed as 'Resolving the activist problem'.

My forehead creased. It was clear that the board had had enough, but while I couldn't blame them, I privately thought that coming up with ways to strike back was not the solution. While the notification didn't exactly spell it out, I had a strong feeling it was what they had in mind.

As always, staff members were invited to attend and contribute to the meeting. I bit my lip, knowing that I would have to go. I at least had to try and curb anything that might get the zoo in even deeper trouble. I only hoped that the rest of the zoo staff would recognise the potential for problems by leaving decisions like this one to a group of people, who for the most part, didn't actually work around the zoo.

I sighed and picked Olive up, intent on leaving the zoo via the main entrance. Perhaps I'd be spotted and shouted at by the protesters, but I refused to be cowed and alter my route. Especially when I was actually in the process of doing something for the good of an animal's health.

My short blonde hair frizzed around my head as I shook it, dispelling such self-righteous notions. What ever happened to enjoying the day-to-day life of working with animals?

A slight smile tugged at my lips. "Nothing's ever that simple, is it?" I said aloud and nearly bumped into Jenna, who was coming round the corner of the corridor.

"Hi. I was just getting coffee," she said. I watched as her eyes darted around, looking anywhere but mine. There was a mobile phone in her hand. I inwardly sighed and wondered who she'd been texting this time. Tiff and I had assumed she must have run out of male staff members who worked at the zoo, having either achieved rendezvous with them, or badgered them enough to know she wouldn't be getting anywhere.

"Having a good day?" I asked out of politeness.

Jenna shrugged. "Busy as usual. I hardly get a minute's rest," she said, and I tried to look suitably sympathetic.

Tiff had informed me that Jenna's colleagues told her tales all the time about how little their supposed manager really did. Her idea of busy was apparently sneaking off on endless coffee breaks to chat to more guys.

I did my best to not take secondhand opinions on board, but the evidence was kind of stacked against her today.

"Hey, you saw the people who broke in, didn't you?" Jenna suddenly brightened. She could smell gossip a mile away.

"Yes, I did," I said, and then didn't know what to add to that. Jenna leant forwards, her eyes managing to widen even further as she did so. "Well, they were wearing balaclavas and they broke in and I told the police I thought they might be trying to poison the animals' food," I continued and Jenna wound her neck back a little. Her folded arms hinted she wasn't satisfied and I could tell she had a hundred and one questions on the tip of her tongue.

I made a show of looking down at my phone screen and pasted a suitably horrified expression on my face. "I said I'd get to the vet at eleven! I'd better run, or I won't make it. See you soon, Jenna!" I said, perhaps a little too cheerily.

In an effort to turn the corner before Jenna could call me back, I sped up, only to jump when I nearly collided with the person coming the other way. It was apparently a day of bad timings all round. After blinking back the surprise I realised I recognised my near miss.

"Alison... hi!" I said. The new shop worker gave me a thin smile and hurried on past. I was about to walk around the corner for real this time when I thought to glance back at Jenna. Although her head was half turned away, I could read on her face that she wasn't at all surprised to find Alison back here at a time when most people were working. If I didn't know any better, I may even have thought she was expecting her.

Olive swung gently in the carrier case, as my footsteps continued down the corridor and back to the public area of the zoo. What business could Jenna and Alison have with each other? Jenna managed the reception, but Alison was a shop and odd job girl, so under the jurisdiction of Tiff. I raised an eyebrow as I briefly considered that perhaps Jenna really had gone through the entire male staff... so now she'd started on the women. I snorted and startled a couple of kids who were peering into the mouse house. While it would be amusing if the queen of gossip became the zoo's next hot topic, I knew Jenna well enough to also know the thought would never cross her mind.

"Come on, Olive. Time to face the music," I muttered as we cleared reception and made it into the car park. I glanced across to my left but to my surprise, only two protesters were there with their placards and they didn't even glance my way. "I guess it's our lucky day," I murmured, before continuing onto the car.

Olive didn't like travelling.

The loud yapping was replaced by the gut wrenching sound of yucking up, with five minutes of driving left to go. I winced and stole a glance down at the car seat, which I'd preemptively covered in a towel. I couldn't see any signs of projectile vomit, but that didn't mean I wouldn't find it, or smell it later.

"You are going on a diet!" I growled when I tipped the ungrateful otter out of the travel box and back into the enclosure that lunchtime. I huffed as she ran off and immediately began chattering to her partner, Popeye.

If I'd been her zookeeper for longer, I knew I wouldn't have made the same mistake. I'd have also figured out a way to stop her from hogging all of the food from poor Popeye, who was definitely dwarfed by his mate's circumference. Of course, now it was down to me to devise some method of feeding them separately. The ghost of a smile lifted my lips. It might seem crazy, but I loved these little challenges.

The zoo seemed conspicuously empty when I walked back through the visitor route. I was hoping there'd be time to grab a sandwich from the fridge before the next round of chores ate away my day. After walking for a few moments more without seeing anyone at all, I started to think it was strange. Mondays were busy days, especially during the summer holidays. Where the heck was everyone?

I instinctively ducked when I heard an enraged screech.

A yellow and black missile shot over my head and landed on one of the sculptural dead trees the zoo had nailed on, to pretty up the outsides of enclosures.

Well that was one mystery solved. The absence of the general public was down to the squirrel monkeys having escaped their enclosure. Now they were out, they would proceed to run rampant, doing what damage they could to both property and people. Until someone unfortunate was assigned the task of catching them dragged them back.

I watched the small, furry face with those two dark, bright eyes that looked back at me from the ex-tree. Dextrous monkey hands kept the squirrel monkey in place and it made inquisitive noises that would lull anyone with less experience into a sense of false security. They might even think they were cute. I'd seen zookeepers with scars that proved otherwise.

"Well, good day to you, small monkey. I'll be on my way now," I said, keeping a wary eye on it as I walked past, hopefully heading out of the danger zone. The primate section of the zoo was further in, although there was always a chance that some of the little scamps had made it this far, even though their keeper should have been hot on their tail. I felt a stab of annoyance but reflected that at least this time they'd evacuated the zoo. Monkeys sought out small children like homing missiles.

My mind was so firmly fixed on the tuna and sweetcorn sandwich I'd spotted earlier in the daily selection within the staff fridge that I nearly bumped into Tom when he appeared from a side gate. His sandy hair was tufted from pulling but his eyes immediately lit up when he saw me. My heart sank like a stone and I relegated all thoughts of lunch.

"Madi, you wouldn't mind rounding up the monkeys for me, would you? I'd have sorted it already but I've got a meeting with the head of the board and I can't miss that. Give it a shot, but they'll probably go back home once they're bored, you know," he said, holding out a net.

I didn't take it.

"Really? You just happen to have a meeting right after the monkeys escape."

His expression morphed into a frown and his bottom lip

jutted out. I was reminded of exactly why I'd refused him when he'd suddenly decided to ask me out the last time we'd spoken. Tom would play whatever character he chose in order to get what he wanted from you.

"What? Do you want me to get him to write a note?" he sneered and let go of the pole of the net, forcing me to catch it. He lifted his chin and looked down on me (something which he didn't actually have to lift his chin to do) before spinning on his heel and making to walk back through the gate he'd appeared through, having found a victim.

"Hey, Tom, how did the monkeys escape?" I called after him and a fresh glower appeared on his face. He opened the gate and slammed it behind him without answering.

"I'm guessing they climbed out using the clematis. Who would have thought?" I looked back the way I'd come. The squirrel monkey started to chatter. He was probably already laughing.

I didn't even bother to chase the monkey I'd already met, although he ran ahead of me all the same as I walked deeper into the zoo. My first port of call was to get rid of that clematis, or the squirrel monkeys would be one short shimmy away from another shot at freedom.

Abandoning the net on the bridge next to the enclosure, I rolled over the side of the bridge, glad that everyone was so studiously avoiding the monkey zone. I ended up hanging by my fingertips with my legs kicking the air in a futile attempt to reach the bank below. In the end, I had to let go and drop, trusting that the bank really was only a couple of inches beneath me. After a brief wobble, I realised everything was okay and I hadn't yet fallen in the river. It was the first thing that had actually gone to plan today, I realised.

I tugged down the tendrils of plant, which the monkeys had clung to on their way out. My eyes scanned the enclosure but I was unsurprised to find it entirely deserted. You had to hand it to the monkeys, when given the chance for freedom, they seized it.

Getting out of the enclosure was harder than getting in and there were several times where I even toyed with the idea of hanging out there all day and claiming I got stuck. It was an almost watertight guarantee that I wouldn't see any squirrel monkeys. The only thing that held me back was the lack of loos and the knowledge that the responsibility for getting the monkeys back rested entirely on me. With the primate specialist at his incredibly convenient 'meeting'. I was the keeper who looked after the odds and ends, which somehow made me next in line. "But I'll be damned if I'm going to do it all alone!" I grumbled, sweating, and no doubt red faced, when I finally managed to roll back over the side of the bridge.

I left the net where it was and instead went to load up on tasty snacks to use as monkey bait. Better to bribe them than boss them. "Time to go see about some recruits," I muttered, stalking deeper into the zoo in search of a posse.

The first part of my search yielded no results. On either side of the walkway, animals looked through the glass viewing windows and I could swear some of them seemed puzzled by the lack of faces looking back in at them.

More concerning was the glaring absence of the escapees. Had they finally managed to escape the confines of the zoo, or were they already creating mischief somewhere?

I almost jumped for joy when I found a person wearing the zoo uniform. She had her back to me and was looking into the otter enclosure. Brown, shoulder-length hair swung around her neck, and I could see her right elbow moving, as though she were writing something down.

"Hi!" I said brightly, making the girl jump. I didn't let my smile falter when I recognised Alison Rowley. Not even when she slipped the notebook into the back pocket of her jeans, so fast she must have hoped I'd missed it.

"Hi," she said, turning her head and looking behind her, clearly keen to get away.

I gritted my teeth and kept up the smile. "You're just the person I need. I know you're great with animals and have some really good knowledge. You've probably heard that the squirrel monkeys have escaped and I really need a hand from someone smart to help me get them back where they belong." I wondered if I was laying it on too thick. "And you've probably also noticed everyone else is hiding." *There,* I thought, as a hint of a smile tweaked Alison's narrow lips.

"I am at a loose end right now, seeing as the zoo is shut. What's the plan?" She flipped her palms upwards and I tried not to seize her hands with gratitude.

"The plan is bribery and if that doesn't work, more bribery," I said, opening the messenger bag I'd filled up with fruits like cherries, strawberries and grapes. I'd actually had to raid the staffroom for some of the bits, but I figured it was the least people could do if they were all going to play hide and seek.

"So, not much of a plan then," Alison observed and in spite of the evidence warning me not to, I found myself warming to her.

"Yep, we're probably going to get our asses handed to us, but maybe by the end of the day we'll have managed to herd them back home." I hoped so anyway. Otherwise I'd be staying late... again. I wondered if Tom would come and lend a hand once his 'meeting' had finished. Somehow I suspected he'd be trotting off to the car park at the end of the day, as quickly as his treacherous legs would carry him.

"Just remember the golden rule... don't be fooled by the cute and furry," I started to say but Alison was already nodding.

"They bite, scratch, and maim. I know," she said with such trepidation that made me think she'd had firsthand experience. Once more, I found myself wondering what someone with so much obvious animal expertise was doing working as a temp odd jobs girl, before I focused on the task at hand. Interrogating my only helper was not in my best interests right now.

"All right, let's go catch some monkeys!" I said, sarcasm on point.

The monkeys remained elusive. With the exception of the lone one I'd spotted before I'd known there was trouble, the main pack had yet to appear. It wasn't until we heard the familiar clamour of construction tools that I spotted one of the escapees, peering over the top of a half-finished boundary fence. Three other monkeys were dotted around the still to be completed capybara enclosure. One was doing something unspeakable to a previously decorative tree.

I wasn't the only one to have spotted the freedom seekers. Rich had quit overseeing his colleagues and was reaching out a hand to the monkey on the fence. The other builders looked on with stupid grins fixed on their faces, as their boss made monkey noises towards the curious squirrel monkey. A couple of the others, Todd and Jack, were trying to get closer to a monkey perched on an excellent example of the zoo's favourite sculptural dead trees. Jack had taken out his phone and Todd was inching closer and closer while they tried to snap a picture.

"Oh dear Lord," I said, exasperated. Unwittingly, my gaze was drawn across to the left, where Lowell was about to haul away another wheelbarrow full of dirt. His dark eyes met mine and seemed to shine with a hidden amusement, as if he knew as well as I did what was coming next. Our shared moment seemed to go on forever, until he nodded once and turned away, leaving me with the strangest sensation in the pit of my stomach.

I almost missed the action.

The squirrel monkey Rich had been making noises at saw something it liked. It jumped and landed neatly on Rich's shoulder. He spread his palms and grinned to his mates. "I'm an animal magnet," he said, just as the monkey seized a tuft of hair and pulled.

Rich screamed.

I couldn't blame him, he didn't have much hair left to lose and the mischievous monkey had just nabbed a fistful of what was left.

"Getoff!" Rich made to swipe the monkey off his shoulder, while his underlings fell about with laughter. The monkey sank its sharp little teeth into his hand. This time his scream was even higher.

"Ouch," Alison commented. We exchanged nods of good luck and stepped into the fray.

In the end, Rich was the only person who lost blood. Jack and Todd's photo taking session was interrupted as soon as Rich started to scream and flail. The other monkeys rushed to help their friend, but sweet treats and swift movement had persuaded them to avert their attack.

"I thought they were the cute fuzzy kind," was all Rich had had to say when the monkeys were led from him. That was probably as much thanks as I was ever going to get.

Once the monkeys knew I had food, they flocked to sit on me and I had to waddle back to their enclosure, clad in furry psychos, who were likely to start scratching and biting as soon as the food ran out.

Alison opened the door to their sleeping compartment

and the monkeys had been unceremoniously dumped back in. The loner had been lurking nearby the enclosure, and after the main offenders had been contained, it wasn't hard to draw him in and put the happy family back together.

"Thanks so much for helping," I said to Alison, once the door was firmly shut behind the monkeys.

"Don't mention it. It beats stacking shelves," she said with a weak smile.

"How come you're doing that job? If you don't mind my asking…" I tilted my head and looked up at her in what I hoped was a non-threatening manner. With our height difference, I probably didn't have to worry.

Alison shrugged. "I just needed something for the summer, while I figure out what to do with my life. I know I'm 26 and probably should have figured it out by now, but…" she gave me a sheepish look and I nodded. I got it. I knew that there were a lot of people, of all ages, who hadn't a clue what they really wanted to do with their lives. I'd always thought it was better to recognise that you weren't in the right job and do something about it - no matter how old you were - than stick at something you hated and wake up to retirement, full of regrets.

I knew I was one of the lucky ones.

"Well, I'm sure you'll figure it out. You probably already know, but you've got a great aptitude for working with animals and your knowledge is impressive, too," I said, and she blushed.

"Thanks," she replied, shifting her weight from foot to foot. I wondered if she'd picked up on the scepticism in my voice. "I'd better be getting back. Tiff will probably wonder where I've been all this time."

"Just tell her you were doing me a favour," I said, pleased to be able to help. She nodded, looking happier, and then gave me a half wave before walking back in the direction of the shops. I watched her go, feeling a crease between my eyebrows.

I knew a lot of people didn't know what they wanted to do with their lives, but I could tell Alison Rowley was definitely not one of them.

"Hey, Madi," Auryn waved from where he'd been chatting to one of the zoo's baristas. She shot me a glare that I pretended not to see. Apparently oblivious, Auryn abandoned her and came over to where I was feeding the lemurs.

"And where were you earlier today?" I asked.

Auryn's smile turned into a grimace. I shot him a look that said I knew exactly where he'd been - hiding with all of the other keepers.

"I heard you did a great job rounding up the monkeys. Apparently Rich finally got what was coming to him, too?" he said, clearly hoping that sweet words would persuade me to forget his absence.

"Yeah, he got bitten pretty badly. I don't think he'll need stitches though," I conceded.

I hadn't actually hung around to find out. When I'd carted the monkeys away, the other builders were still laughing at their boss.

"You've got some new fans. The builders all think you're pretty tough for walking away with all those monkeys, especially after they'd tasted blood," Auryn said, rather melodramatically.

I inwardly raised an eyebrow. Perhaps my newfound respect could come in useful in the near future when I angled again for the changes I wanted made to the capybara enclosure. At the very least, I could threaten to unleash the monkeys again. Although they'd no doubt find their own way out again sooner or later, I thought with a private sigh.

"So where was everyone?" I asked, my earlier annoyance dissipating now the job had been done.

Auryn still looked uncomfortable.

"Oh, you know. People were busy working. I looked in on the bats for a bit, just to make sure they were okay and I think some of the other keepers were cleaning out the ponds…"

"Funny how jobs that have been put off for months suddenly become appealing when the squirrel monkeys escape," I observed.

"Hey, Auryn, do you know why your dad would be having a meeting with Tom today?" I asked, remembering who I was talking to.

He shrugged. "I didn't even think my dad was in today. I don't talk to him that much though." His grey eyes found mine and reminded me of a puppy looking for approval. I suddenly felt bad for assuming he'd know the answer, just because his relatives had control of the zoo. It was exactly the stigma that Auryn probably wanted to escape.

"Well, I reckon I've been had," I said, sharing a smile with him, which - to my relief - he echoed.

"Ah well, you got them all back where they belong. I bet anyone else would have really struggled," he said, and I felt a warm blush rise to my cheeks before I firmly stomped down on the feeling.

"Well, it was luck really. The monkeys were hungry enough to be bribed by the fruit I brought them," I explained, figuring that sharing what had happened might mean I got more help the next time.

"You always have the best ideas," Auryn continued and in spite of telling myself I wasn't going to be flattered, I felt my spirits lift.

"Thanks, Auryn. I'd better get on with feeding the rabble, or I'll be here all night!"

He seemed to shake himself out of a trance, probably realising that he too had duties to fulfil.

"Right, I'll see you later, yeah? Hey, are you going to that board meeting thing?" he said as an afterthought.

I nodded, grimly.

"See you there then." Auryn smiled one more dazzling smile and then walked away.

Dust from the hay swirled in the beams of evening sunlight when I entered the barn behind the zoo. There was the usual panicked scuffling, as the cats ducked for cover. I placed the food tray on the floor and scanned my surroundings. I noticed a few stalks of hay twitching on top of a bale. My feet carried me over as silently as I knew how.

I peered over the top and found myself face to face with the black cat with the white socks. She looked up at me and mewed, but I didn't sense any aggression. I tentatively reached out a hand and stroked her head. She put up with it, only unleashing a halfhearted hiss. I could see her sides moving, as the kittens within started to jostle for freedom. The cat had built herself a cosy nest in the straw.

"Good luck, you'll do fine," I said to the mother-to-be, who looked sceptically back. I shrugged my shoulders. If she wanted fussing over, she'd have stayed home, wherever that was. I knew that cats often went off on their own to have kittens. Unless there were any complications, she'd be fine and I thought it likely that I'd be seeing kittens tomorrow.

"I'll be here first thing," I promised her, before walking back through the barn. It was a rule that was so often hard to keep, but when you were able, you should always let nature take its course.

6

A HIDDEN AGENDA

I t was a fresh Tuesday morning, and the dew still clung to the grass when I made my way to the barn. Long stalks brushed against my jeans, soaking all the way up to my knees, but I knew it would probably be dry by mid-morning. There were a few puffs of white cloud in the sky, but the pale blue stratosphere whispered the promise of yet another beautiful day. Our little corner of England was really lucking out this summer.

I watched the grass ripple as cats fled from my approach. I knew that many of them would be out hunting. With any luck, they'd catch a good few rats and prove their worth.

The barn itself felt quiet when I walked in and set down the food. The hay still held warmth from the previous days of sun and I had a strong urge to drop everything and lie on top of the bales. I rubbed my tired eyes. Perhaps I should wind back on the time I spent working on the comic. I clearly needed some more sleep. "And a day off," I muttered to myself.

I had been getting one day off a week, but since Ray had

died, it had been all hands on deck. The only good thing was getting paid for the overtime and the knowledge that I still had my paid holiday, having not had a moment to even think about using it.

I definitely deserve a treat, I thought, walking over towards the bale the pregnant cat had been behind. Perhaps I would treat myself to a fancy dinner. It had taken years, but I no longer felt bad about going to restaurants on my own. With a good book for company, I'd finally realised people didn't care that I wasn't there with anyone else. The servers never treated me any differently, although, that could be because I was good for business. One dessert was never enough.

I frowned and tugged at the waistband on my jeans. Yep, it was looser than it had been. It was definitely a while since I'd treated myself, and I reckoned I could afford to splash out.

"How are we doing?" I said, hearing the nerves in my voice when I peered over the top of the bale. Two green eyes looked back at me and then narrowed into slits for a few moments. I breathed a sigh of relief. Mother cat seemed to be doing fine, which just left...

I leant further over the bale, having to push up onto my toes and scooch along on my stomach. Three little balls of fur were lined up along her side. I could see an orange and black, an orange and cream, and a black and white. I smiled at the mother cat. "They're very cute."

I was about to turn away and leave her be, when I heard a thin squeaking sound. I looked down at the cat again, but the kittens were all happily nursing. A pile of hay moved and I saw a little black nose poking out, questing for food.

"Did you get lost?"

I wriggled between two hay bales, hoping that this wasn't going to disturb the mother cat too much. With one hand, I scooped the black bundle out of the hay and counted four white socks. This little kitten definitely took after its mum. I gently pushed it towards the nursing cat, noting as I did so that it was smaller than its brothers and sisters. Green eyes met mine again. The cat stuck out a white socked paw and firmly pushed the black kitten away. My heart dropped but the message was clear. *I'm only taking care of these three.*

I chewed my lip, looking down at the lonely kitten. It was all well and good saying that you should let nature take its course, but it was damn difficult when you knew there was something you could do to make a difference. I didn't need another second to think about it. The kitten was scooped up again and dropped into the breast pocket of my work polo shirt. It looked like I'd just inherited a cat.

Fortunately, I'd come in super early to visit the cat, so I had plenty of time to pop across to the vet and pick up some kitten milk formula and a few pieces of advice. It was one thing being a zookeeper and caring for animals that you'd studied for years and there was a ton of inter-zoo shared information on, but quite a different thing to care for a kitten without a mother. In some ways, it was simpler. I didn't have to worry about having too much human contact, as if all went to plan, we were going to be friends for a very long time. In other ways, I knew there would be challenges. Looking after an entirely dependent kitten wasn't exactly in my job description, so I was going to have to be pretty careful about who I told, or risk being called out for spending too much time on something that wasn't work. I smirked, as I considered pretending I'd taken up smoking. That always seems to justify multiple breaks.

"How's that then?" I said to the black and white kitten. I'd put the formula into a dropper and was gently squeezing it, so the kitten could eat what it wanted. Once that was done, I damped a clean cloth and helped it go to the loo. Motherly duties complete, I found a small carrying case, no bigger than a lunch box, and made a soft nest, perfect for a kitten.

There was a bundle of soft toys that had been donated to use to comfort young animals that had been rejected by their parents. I selected a yellow fuzzy duck and popped it into the carrier for a snuggle buddy.

"Better get started on our rounds," I said to the little ball of fur, who had immediately fallen asleep next to the duck. While it was early days, I suspected I had a little boy cat on my hands. I knew I should really start thinking of names, but somehow it felt unlucky to do it so soon. *I'll give it a few days,* I thought to myself. Plenty of time to come up with something.

I hadn't told anyone about the barn cat's pregnancy, so no one suspected a thing when I went about the usual daily chores with a furry friend in tow. I guessed anyone who saw the little travel case probably thought I was taking my lunch for a walk.

The only person I shared the news with was Tiff, when she met me during her coffee break.

"Hey, do you want to meet my new friend?" I said, picking up the carrier to show her. Tiff eyed it nervously for a moment until I told her it was a kitten. In hindsight, I couldn't blame her. In a zoo where some people thought giant cockroaches were cute, you never knew what you were about to come face to face with.

"He's so little!" she said, when I took the kitten out to feed it some more formula. I checked his temperature too, but the day, although warm, was not excessively hot. My new partner seemed happy enough.

"His brothers and sisters are still in the barn with their mother. I'll have to catch them all when they're the right age to be neutered. The mother, too," I said with a sigh. The kitten's mother may not be a bonafide feral by my judgement, but her offspring were going to be 100% wild. It was always a barrel of joy when you had to catch a cat to prevent the population from exploding.

"I'd come and see them, but I know disturbing them is bad. Although, if the mother did decide she doesn't want any of her other kittens, I could probably squeeze another pet in somewhere," Tiff said with a smile.

Her house was already overrun with waifs and strays. While I'd managed to swerve rescue duties over the years (until now) Tiff had a soft spot for anything orphaned and furry.

I was supremely pleased that Tiff hadn't asked to see the other kittens. It reassured me that the cat would remain undisturbed. Even seasoned zookeepers could go a bit baby-crazy. With the rumour mill being what it was, the poor cats would be inundated by lunchtime if I didn't keep my mouth shut.

"Is that a kitten?" A deep voice said.

I found myself staring into a familiar pair of dark eyes and for a second I knew I'd forgotten to breathe.

Tiff nudged me when I didn't reply.

"A kitten, yes. It came from the cat barn, you know…" I trailed off. Lowell wasn't supposed to have been anywhere near there. I deliberately didn't look at Tiff and hoped she'd forget it. "Would you mind not telling anyone about it? I know it's just a kitten but I really don't want the mother to be bothered, or we may lose them all," I said, as tactfully as I could.

Lowell nodded, brusquely. He glanced at Tiff, but I noticed it wasn't the usual besotted look that most men threw in her direction. It was almost as if he wished she wasn't standing there.

Another pause morphed into a silence and I felt my

cheeks warm. Tiff started looking back and forth between us, before Lowell finally turned and walked away.

"Who is **that**?" Tiff hissed in delight, the second he was out of earshot. Or almost out of earshot anyway.

"He's the new builder. I don't know him or anything," I said, wondering why I was making excuses.

Tiff gave a sceptical look. "Sure," she said but couldn't keep the smile from bursting free. "Well, well, well! Does this mean you're finally coming out of the dating doldrums? He's so tall! It'll be like climbing a tree..." She broke off when I battered her with my hands to make her shut up. "Using the cute kitten to get the guy to talk to you... I like it. All this time, you had me wondering. But you've known how to play the game all along, you sly minx!"

"The game?" I said, blankly.

"The game," Tiff confirmed, nodding like this conversation wasn't absolute nonsense. "Just remember, you promised me I could be bridesmaid."

"At my imaginary, never-gonna-happen wedding," I reminded her. "Unless I marry myself, don't plan on going dress shopping any time soon."

"I heard there's a growing trend for that sort of thing," Tiff commented.

"How wonderful to know that spinsterhood is now trendy," I replied, drenching it in sarcasm.

Tiff just snorted.

"Are you going to the meeting later?" I asked, deciding it was high time I diverted the conversation to more sensible affairs. I placed the kitten back in its carrier and it returned to cuddling up with the toy duck.

"No, I'm just going to go home. I never know what to say at those meetings and while you know I support you, all of this protest stuff doesn't have a lot to do with the shop. I think people would probably think I was being super overcontrolling if I tried to get in on it. Plus Erin Avery gives me the creeps."

Erin Avery, son of Mr Avery Senior, and divorcee father to Auryn, was the head of the board of directors. He'd always seemed like an okay kind of guy to me, but someone like Tiff had an unfortunate tendency to occasionally bring out the sides of a person you didn't always see. Especially if the person was male. She pulled a face at me and I shuddered. He probably was just your average guy deep down, but for someone in his fifties to be chasing after Tiff was definitely uncomfortable.

"I'll see you when I see you then," I said to her with a smile.

"Yes, although, you'll probably be sick of me soon. It's not that I'm not crazy about you Madi, but now you have that cute little bundle, I'll seek you out like Madi chasing down a chocolate cake," she said with a grin that made her nose crease up in a sickeningly attractive way.

"Uh, Tiff, using similes that have me as the subject when you're having a conversation with me is weird."

"Oh, sorry. I guess I just use that one so much, it slipped out," Tiff said with an evil grin.

I wasn't sure if she was joking.

The meeting had already started when I made it to the zoo's restaurant. Just beyond the foyer was the conference room where board meetings were held.

One of the bats had been reported behaving erratically and I'd had to observe it for a while, which was why I was a little late. I didn't think there was anything seriously wrong, but every time something was reported, it had to be checked.

"Remember you promised me you'll stay quiet," I whispered to the little kitten I carried by my side. I'd really have to hope people assumed the carrier was my lunchbox.

Erin Avery had just finished some sort of opening speech, when I inched my way into the back of the room. His blonde thatch of hair hadn't thinned a bit and I thought Auryn's prospects looked pretty good if that was the way the Avery men aged. I couldn't vouch for his mother, as she and Erin had divorced long before I'd joined the zoo. While Erin still retained a few of the hallmarks that hinted he had once been a handsome man, that didn't justify him behaving in any manner that would make Tiff feel uncomfortable. I glowered for a second and hoped it was a long time in the past. I may be small, but I was also fierce and I felt protective of my friends.

"Now before we take a vote, shall we adjourn for refreshments?" Mr Avery said.

I blinked. Had I missed more of the meeting than I'd imagined? What had just been proposed? I turned to the person next to me, a man I vaguely recognised from the caretakers' team, but he shushed me before I could speak. Next to him, Colin, the keeper in charge of equine and hoofed animals rolled his eyes.

I bit my tongue. I'd have to find someone else to explain what was going on. What on earth could have been proposed in the first five minutes that needed a vote?

I took a step towards the refreshments table, trying to ignore the allure of a large, sticky toffee cake. A loud squeak cut through the air and I jumped. At least three pairs of eyes turned to look at me. Coughing loudly and miming a bad throat, I retreated back into the foyer. Knowledge and cake was calling my name, but I was worried there was something seriously wrong with my youngest charge.

"What's the matter?" I asked, once we were clear of the foyer and in the evening air. He mewled some more and I reached into my messenger bag for the ready mixed formula. I tried a dropper full, and he eagerly latched on. "Huh! Seems like you and I share a fondness for filling our bellies. Now, we'll just go back in…" I turned around to face the restaurant.

The bomb went off before I could take a step.

7

LUCKY

T he outer foyer windows shattered when the force of the blast hit them and I staggered, my body instinctively shielding the kitten's carrier. A few fragments of glass sliced my arms as they flew by, but in the dazed moments that followed, I couldn't detect any life-threatening injury. My ears were ringing. I knew I probably wasn't thinking straight, but I stowed the kitten's carrier under a bush and ran back into the building.

It was like something from a disaster movie. I could hear the groans and cries of those who had been caught in the blast, muffled by my damaged eardrums. Worse, were the bodies lying here and there that made no sound at all. *What happened?* My brain uselessly repeated.

I saw one woman trying to get to her feet, her face streaked with debris and hurried to help her out of the building. Once she was out, I did it again and again, until the police and the ambulances arrived. I spared a thought to wonder who had called them and realised that should have been the first thing I'd done.

A paramedic came up to me and looked at the cuts on my

arm. I waved him away, knowing that there were people who needed his help far more urgently than I did. A lot of people.

I wondered how many of them I knew.

I wondered how many of them were dead.

"Excuse me please," I said to a passing police officer. She looked harried and her brown hair was flying free from her french plait, but she stopped all the same. "It was a bomb that did this, right?" I asked.

She bit her lip. "We can't say so soon, but…" She left it hanging. We'd both seen the casualties carried out with nuts and bolts embedded in them. This was no gas explosion.

I sat down by the bush where I'd left the kitten and pulled his little carrier onto my lap. I spent a moment checking him, but he was sound asleep, his little belly moving up and down rhythmically. It was only then that I realised he'd probably saved my life, or at the very least, saved me from grievous injury.

"Pretty Lucky, huh?" I said, and smiled, knowing I'd already found his name.

I was still smiling when the police officer came over. Fortunately, she must have passed it off as shellshock, as she didn't comment on my inappropriate facial expression.

"I'm so sorry to bother you, but we're talking to all witnesses able to give a statement." She pointed and I followed her finger to where a group of dusty and disheveled people were sat on the plastic outdoor chairs. They were all staring into space with empty looks of disbelief on their faces. I knew the feeling.

"Sure," I said, making my way over with a heavy heart. The ambulances had been coming and going for a while, but the stream had stopped when no one was left inside. I'd over-heard one of the medics say that we were lucky the structure of the building had held up, so at least no one had been buried. With the exception of me, I doubted anyone was feeling that lucky right now.

I nodded to Katrina, one of the receptionists, and she nodded back, before returning to her vigil of staring blankly at nothing. My manager, Morgan, sat next to her. His eyes met mine but we stayed silent. Words didn't seem right. I realised the ringing in my ears had faded to a distant hum, which was something at least.

I gave my statement. The officer finished writing down everything I'd said about what I'd seen but I felt like it wasn't enough. He wasn't asking the right questions.

"You know what this meeting was about, don't you?" I said.

The young officer raised his eyebrows, enquiringly.

"It was looking at ways we could stop the animal rights activists from interfering with the zoo. They've been protesting ever since the serval died after eating a poisoned rat. We've had a zookeeper die under some pretty suspicious circumstances, a car vandalised, and then a break-in, where I think the activists were trying to interfere with animal food supplies to make the zoo look even worse." I took a breath while the officer scribbled away. It was typical bureaucracy. He probably hadn't a clue about any of the other cases and how they all connected.

"And you think this attack has something to do with all of that?" he asked. I saw him immediately bite his tongue afterwards.

"Yes, I do. I think it's probably a group of extremists who are responsible. They're here and they're willing to kill people in order to close the zoo down." They might have just succeeded, too, I suddenly realised. If they'd managed to take out the head of the board of directors and son of the zoo owner, Erin Avery, they may have achieved their aims.

I looked around at the ragged bunch of people, but didn't

recognise the blonde hair of Erin Avery, even covered with dust.

I tried to remember the moments before the bomb had gone off. He'd announced a refreshment break and I remembered him walking out a side door. Had he made it to safety, or had the blast caught him?

"When will you know more about what happened?" I asked the young officer.

"We've got a team of bomb specialists coming in and we'll of course be keeping everyone updated." He looked at me with his serious green eyes. "Don't you worry, we'll catch the people who did this," he said, and by gosh, I thought he probably believed what he was saying.

I did my best to make my lips curve up and keep the sigh inside.

They hadn't figured out what had happened to Ray, uncovered the identity of the car vandals, or caught the two men who'd broken in. What would make this incident any different? All fingers were pointing at the culprits and still they were slipping away.

A flash of anger burrowed through me when I wondered what damage had been done today. How many were dead? How many were injured? How could anyone profess to love animals and then do something like this to other human beings?

"It's a mad world we live in," I said to the little kitten, who woke up and squeaked his agreement.

"You can go home now, if you think you'll be okay getting yourself home?" The officer said, reappearing after conferring with his seniors.

"I'll be fine," I said, suddenly wanting to be anywhere but here. I wanted to get home and jump in the shower to wash away all the filth of the aftermath of the bomb. It wouldn't be enough. I'd seen so many bad things this evening. I knew they would stick with me for a long time... probably forever.

I barely noticed the drive home. I was just numb. I knew I'd seen dead bodies, but I had no idea who they were. I was sure by tomorrow, everyone would know the truth.

I thought about calling around people I knew, but everyone was probably doing the same. I'd already been texted by Tiff, Auryn, Lucy, and Leah, asking if I was okay. I'd replied with the affirmative. Jenna had also texted, but had been asking after juicy details rather than my wellbeing. I hadn't bothered to respond to that message.

"You've had quite a first day of life, Lucky," I said to the black and white ball of fluff, who was settled in my hand. I stroked him a few times and then returned him to the warm comfort of the toy duck. Despite all the drama, he seemed just fine.

Running on autopilot, I sat down at my desk and looked at the blank comic strip in front of me. I'd been in the process of documenting the squirrel monkeys' adventure but the idea of drawing a caricature of Rich being attacked didn't seem as hilarious as it had last night.

I opened up my comic's web page and posted up a guest comic I had in reserve. That would do to keep the fans happy.

I tilted my head, remembering I now had fans. It was still so strange to me. I flicked across to my email inbox where another four messages from people who'd read my comic awaited. After a moment's hesitation, I left them unopened. I felt bad about making people who'd taken the time to write to me wait, but I was done with today. What I needed now was a massive hot chocolate - mostly consisting of cream and marshmallows - and bed.

After going to all of the trouble to put together the incredibly indulgent hot chocolate therapy, I realised I wasn't tired anymore. My body had passed through the exhaustion stage and was now running on adrenaline. I sighed as I thought about lying down on the bed and gave it up as a lost cause. Instead, I sat in front of my computer and did something I should have done days ago.

"Lowell…" I muttered, searching Facebook. It soon came up with a profile that only showed updates going back a couple of months. I raised an eyebrow. Lowell Forrester was looking shadier by the second. I ran a few more searches and came up with nothing, which in this day and age was throwing up all kinds of red flags.

On the off chance, I copied his profile picture and pasted it into Google. I promised myself this would be the full extent of my snooping. If Tiff could see me now, she'd probably say I was acting like a lovestruck teenager, or professional stalker (similar). I told myself it was nonsense. I was just trying to check he was who he claimed to be, simply because he'd been turning up in the strangest places. Tiff's voice whispered that perhaps it was because he was doing everything in his power to get close to me. Those foolish thoughts faded away when the image search loaded.

There was only one match, and it was from this web page that Lowell had so unwisely selected his current Facebook profile picture.

"Rogers and Riordan Private Detectives, Lowell Adagio," I read the caption below the picture on the website. "Well… that explains a lot," I said aloud. In truth, I was more confused as ever. So Lowell was a private detective. Who had hired him and what had he been hired to investigate?

"I think Lowell and I need to have a chat," I said to Lucky, who was hungry again. Hopefully, I was the first person to have tried that Google image search trick. If not, Lowell was probably in serious danger.

The zoo was subdued the next morning. The ongoing investigation and the shocking turn of events meant Avery Zoo was closed to the public, but the keepers still had to go in. Animals didn't stop needing to be cared for when the doors closed to the public. As a result, there was only a skeleton staff working and everyone walked around with heads dipped low, looking solemn. It was only when I found Leah in the staffroom with tears running down her cheeks that I heard the final damage report.

"Hey, are you okay?" I said, sinking into a grey seat next to her. I awkwardly reached my arm up to rest across her shoulders.

She blinked tears from her big eyes and rubbed a hand across her cheeks, smudging foundation. "I'm sorry, it's just so terrible. I can't believe that Colin is gone. He wasn't the friendliest keeper here, but he was a character. He was a part of this zoo and now he's dead... murdered," Leah said, her voice suddenly filling with anger.

"Colin's dead?" I said, softly, reeling when I remembered he'd been stood pretty much right next to me in the meeting.

Leah nodded. "Yeah. Him and two other members of the board. So many people are injured. Vanessa's got stitches all the way up her arm, but she still came in today to look after those stupid insects and slimy things..." A strange laugh bubbled from Leah's throat and the tears dried up for a second.

"Have the police arrested anyone yet?" I asked, wondering if Leah had heard any more.

She shook her head and her irises seemed to grow darker. "No, they haven't. They say they're still investigating who might have had a cause to plant the bomb." She turned to me, her eyes completely dry. "We all know who did it. It's those activists. They've finally gone too far and now people are dead. Why don't the police care?" she said, and I heard the anger of so many of the zoo's staff echo in her voice.

"I'm sure they'll find the people who did this," I said, feeling like I was now playing the role of the police officer who'd told me much the same last night. I wasn't naive enough to truly believe it.

"Hey guys," Leah said as Tom, James, and Lucy, all walked into the staffroom. They sat down near us, no one really saying anything.

Morgan poked his head around the door and and asked if anyone could cover for Colin, before he became so choked up he talked himself into doing the round himself, to honour the keeper's memory.

"Were any of you at the meeting last night?" Tom asked, while Lucy went off to get everyone teas and coffees. The animals were having to wait a little longer for their breakfasts this morning. I glanced down at Lucky's carrier, but he was sound asleep, and no one was in any shape to notice the little kitten inside.

When I looked up again, the other keepers were shaking their heads.

"I think only Vanessa and Colin were there. They usually like to have a say," Leah said, smiling sadly.

"I was there, too, but I arrived late and then ducked out to get some fresh air right before the blast," I said. Everyone stared at me. I self-consciously rubbed the cuts on my forearms, caused by flying glass.

"Wow, Madi! You sure are queen of being in the wrong place at the wrong time. First you find Ray, then you walk in on those people breaking in, when it's not even feeding time, and now you almost got blown up," Tom said, shaking his sandy head. "How unlucky can you get?"

"I don't know. I'm still here, aren't I?" I said, trying to put on a brave face.

In truth, I was rattled. Colin had been right there. He'd been right there! It was not a stretch to put myself in his position. *Although no one should have died at all!* I furiously reminded myself, redirecting my feelings towards the perpetrators of the crime.

"I really hope they find whoever did it," Leah said, speaking for us all.

"Did you hear? Erin Avery got away without so much as a scratch. He left for the bathroom right before the bomb blast and the walls protected him," Lucy said.

That must have been why he called the break - he needed the loo, I thought. Erin Avery was probably counting his lucky stars right now, same as I was.

The unusual quietness of the weekday made it drag on and the few people that were working at the zoo that day seemed to be avoiding each other. We all needed our space to process the terrible thing that had happened.

I'd thought that the press would be knocking down the door as early as that morning, but somehow, it was being kept quiet. The only report I'd seen in the local paper was that the zoo was shut today due to an incident, but that was the only detail. It didn't mention what was essentially a terrorist attack that had stolen lives. I wondered just how long they could sit on the news before it exploded.

I winced.

Not the best choice of words, even to think.

Lucky was doing just fine in his carrier, so I decided to check on his brothers and sisters. The mother cat was in the same place and everyone looked healthy. There'd probably been bedlam when the cats had heard the blast, but I saw no lasting effects. I was glad that the restaurant was way over the other side of the zoo, so there was no chance of emergency services coming here.

I took a few moments out to sit on a hay bale. There was less to do than normal because the public weren't around and I needed some time to reflect. There were so many thoughts swirling around in my head, I knew I had to put a few in order. I was sure there was important information right in front of me that I wasn't seeing. The answers were there, I just needed to open my eyes.

My thoughts drifted to Lowell and his secret. The builders weren't working today and I wondered what he was up to right now. Did he know who was behind the attacks? Had he been hired to find out who murdered Ray, or was his job to take down the animal rights extremists?

With everything else that happened, it was obvious Ray's death was no tragic accident. But even with that knowledge, I was still no closer to figuring out why anyone would specifically go after the penguin keeper. Had his death merely been opportunism, or had he known something that had meant he'd had to die? Perhaps he'd known who was working for the activists inside the zoo...

Alison Rowley and her suspiciously comprehensive knowledge of animals popped into my head. Yes, she'd saved my bacon when I'd needed help catching the squirrel monkeys, but I didn't think I'd be able to forgive her if she was a part of the bomb plot. Was it as I suspected, and she was currently working as an inside woman for the activists? I chewed my lip, knowing I should probably go to the police with a piece of information like that. The thing was, I still wanted to give her a chance. It was nuts, but I thought I'd try and question her myself before getting the police involved. Even if she was an activist, I knew better than to tar them all with the same brush. She may not be an extremist.

It was a complicated situation that seemed to be spiralling further and further out of control.

I was in the bat enclosure again when Auryn found me. I'd been observing Amelie, the bat who'd been acting strangely recently, and I now wasn't so sure everything was okay. She didn't seem to be gripping the branches as dextrously as her kin, and her coat definitely lacked lustre.

I was on the verge of climbing over the fence for a closer look when the plastic flaps parted.

"Hey Madi, are you okay? I'm so sorry you were there when it happened," Auryn said, and suddenly looked sheepish. "I know I said I was going. I was going to turn up before the end... I just thought the first half would be my dad's usual waffle."

"I'm glad you missed the action," I said to him, finding it comforting to see his golden face unmarred by shrapnel. "Is your dad okay?" I asked while Auryn bent down and examined Lucky's carrier. I smiled to myself, secretly pleased that he was so observant. It boded well for his ambitions to become a zookeeper.

"There's a kitten in there!" he said, and tilted his head in a 'may I?' gesture. I nodded and he gently scooped up the sleeping kitten.

"One of the feral cats rejected him, so I took him in. He started crying for food about ten seconds before the bomb exploded. That was why I was outside when it happened," I told him.

He turned white.

"I didn't realise you were that close to it."

"I had a lucky escape, thanks to Lucky here," I said, but my smile was wan. The disaster hung heavy in the air.

Auryn returned Lucky to his carrier and the kitten continued to snuffle in what passed for a tiny snore.

He lowered his grey eyes to meet mine, giving me a look so serious it made him appear far older than his nineteen years. "If anything happened to you, Madi, I don't know what I'd do."

"Oh, Auryn, I'm okay. I just wish nobody had got hurt at all," I said, feeling a lump in my throat as I thought about poor old Colin. It made what happened to his car seem like nothing at all.

"I just never want to lose you," Auryn said. I looked back up at him in time to see him leaning forwards.

The next second we were kissing.

I froze up for a moment when his lips pressed against mine, hard and urgent, and then softening as I melted into the kiss, willing myself to forget everything else that had happened. Something tapped away at the back of my mind until I pulled away. He gave me a confused look and I blushed, knowing I was probably well on my way to looking like a blonde beetroot.

"Auryn, I really like you and I think you're great but this is just a reaction to the scary events that have happened," I said, playing the part of the rational adult.

He shook his pale blonde head of hair. "You don't get it. I've liked you for ages, Madi. This isn't just because of all the bad stuff. I'm really into you," he said. I noticed his cheeks warming and he looked the least cool I'd ever seen him look. Even blushing, he was handsome as ever.

Oh boy, was it hard to say no.

"I am so tempted," I said, figuring honesty was the best policy here, "but I'm not exactly girlfriend material. I'm too old and boring. You need someone closer to your own age who wants to go out and have fun. My idea of a great night is hot chocolate and webcomics," I said, and blushed anew, knowing I was probably being a little too candid.

He gave me a solemn look. "I still think you're the one I'm waiting for, but I guess I'll have to wait a little longer. I can do that," he said, reaching out and pushing a wild strand of my hair behind my ear before I could stop him. "I'll see you around," he said, shooting me a smile that made my stomach do flips in spite of all I'd said.

I opened my mouth to say something - anything - sensible, but he'd already disappeared back through the plastic flaps.

"What just happened?" I said aloud, but the bats had no answer for me.

8

COWS AND CRIMINALS

The zoo reopened a day later. News of the bomb going off had finally been released, but it was still downplayed, probably because the board had realised people might not visit a zoo where things exploded. They'd obviously decided not to give the perpetrators their publicity.

While I respected that, I felt the loss of the three who had died and the multiple people whose lives had been changed by their injuries and the harrowing experience. They deserved recognition but all I could do was make sure that I remembered them.

Morgan's initial emotional offer of aid had lasted all of a single day. It was Thursday and the care of Colin's animals had been divided between the keepers, despite us still struggling with Ray's roster. I'd landed the miniature ponies and the Jersey cows, which suited me fine. It meant a lot of time spent mucking out, but I always found tasks like that were good for reflection.

My view on landing an easy addition changed somewhat

when I found Colin's notes and discovered that a female Jersey was due to give birth, pretty much any minute now.

"Great. Everyone's having babies," I muttered. Colin had also written that the cow had experienced difficulties during her last pregnancy, so would need careful monitoring. This wasn't a time to just let nature take its course.

I sighed but was inwardly grateful to Colin for making notes, the same way I assumed he'd done when he'd been a farmer. It meant that animals were all accounted for and meticulously kept track of. It was such a great system, I found myself wishing that Ray had kept better records and made a mental note to start keeping my own, too. Drawing comics of amusing zoo happenings didn't really count.

We'd had rain earlier in the day, but the sun was warm on my back that evening when I decided it was time to muck out both the ponies and the cows. Once everything was spick and span I knew I'd feel that I'd properly taken on the care of these new animals.

Now three days old, Lucky was growing more adventurous, and I knew pretty soon I'd have to upgrade his pet carrier. I briefly wondered how I would manage to keep it unnoticed and concluded that (once a little less dependent) Lucky would have to wait in the dependent animals room with the other babies. He squeaked about his empty belly and I fed him some formula while I contemplated the messy task ahead.

"Vanessa, how are you doing?" I called, when the insect enthusiast stalked by.

The older keeper looked up and sighed, her face marked by grief. "As well as can be expected, I suppose. I miss Colin," she admitted, looking over at one of the cows with both fondness and disgust on her face.

I nodded, not knowing what to say. Colin had been an

acquired taste, but as the more senior keepers at the zoo, he and Vanessa had stuck together.

"Of course, I'm now stuck looking after some truly foul pigs, so I don't know how long that feeling will last for," she continued, a thin smile appearing and vanishing in a second. I replied with my own smile and she hesitated for a moment longer before walking off. My eyes slid to the broad, messy stitches that held together a violent gash on her arm.

When did this zoo turn into a war zone? I wondered.

<hr />

It was only after the final round of the evening, just after the zoo had closed, that I admitted to myself I wasn't going home. Amelie the bat hadn't improved. I'd decided I would catch her and do what I could to look after her until we could go to the vet tomorrow. In hindsight, I probably should have taken her before the vets had shut, but I just couldn't figure out what was wrong. She stumbled around the branches like she was as blind as, well… a bat. I'd sensed it wouldn't be long before she plummeted to the ground and did herself a real injury.

There was also the cow conundrum. I'd been watching Blossom, the very pregnant cow, all the time I'd spent cleaning up the paddock and had reached the conclusion that she was definitely in labour. An all night vigil at the zoo beckoned.

"How about we grab ourselves some snacks and settle in?" I said to Lucky, who squeaked whenever he heard my voice. I gently stroked his little head and placed him safely in a little pen in the dependent animal room, making for the staffroom on my own. I hoped there would still be a few sandwiches and bits left over from lunch.

I'd just got my hands on a fairly respectable looking

cream cheese and ham sandwich, when Lowell appeared. He moved so fast it made me jump and I could tell by the way his eyes widened that I'd surprised him, too. You seldom saw a man flat out sprint, like their life depended on it, but that was exactly what Lowell had been doing.

"Please, you've got to hide me," he said, lifting a hand off his shoulder and glancing down. It came away red. My breath caught in my throat.

"What's happening?" I asked, starting to feel a low buzz of fear in my belly. We'd only just started to come to terms with the bombing and now it was happening again.

"They're after me and if they catch me they'll kill me. Do you know where I can go?" he said, and I finally registered what he was saying. Lowell may be bleeding out, but he was in a better mental state than I was.

"Get in the cloakroom. I'll lock it behind you," I said.

He hurried into the tiny room, where all lost property was flung. Usually the key sat in the keyhole, but I swiftly turned it and pocketed it. Now, even if they tried the door, I hoped they'd assume it had been locked all along.

It was only after I'd locked it that I wondered if I should be in the cloakroom with him. If he thought his life was in danger, why did he think I would be fine? Or perhaps he knew exactly what he was doing and I was about to become a victim…

There was no time to do anything other than hope for the best and act like nothing was wrong. I plumped down in a grey chair, just as I heard the heavy fall of running footsteps approaching. Rich, Gary, and Todd tore into the staffroom and ground to a halt when they saw me. I arranged my expression into a confused frown.

"Is something happening?" I asked, hoping I looked calm and not as flustered as I felt.

The men all exchanged glances before Gary spoke.

"We decided to work a little late in order to get a bit of the enclosure done. Once you get started with quick drying cement, you can't stop. We heard someone nearby and went to find out who they were. The zoo's closed, so we figured no one else would have a right to be here," Gary said, like he was explaining it to a two year old. He raised an eyebrow at me.

"I'm here to monitor a sick bat and keep an eye on a cow who may be having a difficult birth," I coolly explained.

"You weren't down by the monkey enclosure a few seconds ago?" Rich asked, sceptically, and Gary nudged him.

"Come on! She's tiny! It was definitely a man, and whoever it was would be pretty out of breath. Maybe hurt, too," he added.

"Someone's hurt?" I asked, and uncomfortable looks were shared.

"Uh, we saw some blood on the side of an enclosure. Maybe the guy breaking in got cut when they heard us come after them," Rich said.

That didn't sound anything like the truth, but I kept my doubts to myself.

"Have you called the police?" I asked and there was more shuffling of feet. I tried not to look as alarmed as I felt. Something bad was going on here and I'd inadvertently landed right in the middle of it.

It was then I noticed a dark spot of blood on the glass coffee table. It must have fallen from Lowell when he'd first arrived in the staffroom. As casually as I could, I placed my sandwich neatly over the blood spot. "Well, if you haven't called the police yet, I think I should probably do that. It could be someone trying to plant another bomb, or go after another zookeeper." My blood chilled when I thought of that possibility. Here I was, spending the night alone at the zoo, when the last keeper who had stayed late wound up at the bottom of the penguin pool. It wasn't one of my smartest ideas.

"You're sure you didn't see anything?" Rich asked again.

I shook my head. "No, but before you guys ran in, I heard someone run by in the direction of reception. I just figured it was someone who lost track of time and didn't want to miss their dinner." I raised my eyes to meet each of the men in turn, ignoring the way my skin crawled. "I'm sure glad you're all around though. Anything might have happened to me if you hadn't chased him off."

"That's okay, we're just doing our bit to keep the zoo safe," Rich said, and Gary flashed me a smile.

I felt sick.

"Are you all going to keep on looking? I really don't mind calling the police," I said, aware that the men were now just standing there, staring at me. They were also starting to look around more carefully, and I really didn't want them to spot any signs Lowell had left behind that I might have missed.

"We'll give them a call, Madi. I think we're going to be heading out. We scared that guy off pretty good. You should be fine here tonight," Rich said, and the others nodded before finally filing back out of the staffroom.

I waited until their footsteps had fully faded, and then another five minutes more, before I let Lowell out of the cupboard.

"Thank you so much…" he started to say, but I folded my arms and gave him a look that made him shut up.

"You need to explain yourself, Lowell Adagio," I said.

He frowned when he heard his real name.

"Right. How did you…?"

"I'll tell you once you've told me everything I want to know," I said to him, casting an anxious glance over my shoulder. I was nearly certain that the lynch mob had given up and gone home, but I still didn't want to take the risk of talking to Lowell in such an accessible area.

"Come with me. We can talk in the dependent animal unit," I told him.

We managed to make it there without incident. Now that the builders had disappeared, the zoo was quiet, with the exception of the noises of the nocturnal animals waking up and the diurnals preparing for bed.

"How much do you know?" Lowell asked, as soon as I'd shut the door after us.

I hesitated before answering, still not sure if I was helping the bad guy, or the good guy.

"I'm working for Mr Avery Senior, if that helps at all," Lowell added and a lot of things started to make sense.

"You're a private detective. A search with your photo on the internet was enough for me to figure that out. You should really do something to fix that," I told him and he nodded humbly. "I know that the zoo is being attacked and the police don't seem to be able to do a thing to stop it, or find whoever is responsible." I paused, thinking before I continued to mindlessly recite the 'facts' that were circulating the zoo right now. "Supposedly, there's a group of animal rights extremists who are out to get everyone at the zoo, and will do anything to shut it down, including killing people and poisoning animals to prove a point," I said, slowly, working it out as I went. "But if that were the whole truth, why would you have been spying on Rich and the builders? I could be wrong, but they don't strike me as the animal activist type. So, why are you investigating them?"

Lowell's dark eyes looked amused and I could have sworn there was even a hint of pride there.

"There is more to this situation than meets the eye, at least, that's what I've figured out so far. The animal rights activists are being used as a front for a gang of criminals to hide behind. Criminals with a very different set of goals," he explained. "Mr Avery hired me to investigate after he noticed something odd, but I still haven't got enough evidence. That was why I took the risk and tried to listen in on the little meeting they were having after hours. Normally on a job, I bug the places where I know that the people I'm watching will meet and talk, but this work is all outside. I have to think on my feet. I was hiding next to the squirrel monkey enclosure using my phone to record them, but one of the monkeys saw me and started screeching. I ran for it, but got caught on one of those damn trees, which tore my shoulder open." He looked down, remembering for the first time that he'd been injured.

I grabbed the first aid box from the wall and laid out the supplies for cleaning him up. He willingly lifted his torn shirt up over his head and I tried not to think too hard about all of those muscles on his tanned torso.

"Did you hear anything good?" I asked, as I tried to be professional and focused on disinfecting the wound.

"I heard a lot and none of it good. They were the ones who set the bomb," he said.

I stopped dabbing with the antiseptic wipe and looked up into his solemn face. "You're serious? They're the ones who killed people?"

"Yes. Gary's the one who made the bomb. I heard him say he used to dabble with stuff like making napalm when he was a kid. With the internet being what it is these days, it's not exactly rocket science to figure out how to put together a bomb, especially when you're working at a place where you can order all kinds of agricultural supplies without anyone batting an eyelid." Lowell winced as I removed a bit of grit.

"You've got to go to the police with what you know. They need to be arrested! Did they kill Ray as well?" I asked, still mightily confused as to why the builders had decided to go on a killing spree.

"I think they might have had something to do with it. Although I don't know for sure." He sighed and I taped up the wound before covering it with a gauze pad.

I made to remove my hand but he reached out and grabbed it before I could take it back.

"I know this is bad but I really need you to trust me. We're going to have to wait just a little bit longer before getting the police involved."

"Why? They need to be stopped before they do something else. Lowell, you said they were going to kill you if they found you tonight," I reminded him.

"It's not a good situation and I'm really sorry that you're a part of this because it means you're in danger, too." He ran a hand through his thick, dark hair. "Something big is about to go down, but the less you know, the better. That way if anything happens…" He trailed off, but I wasn't buying it.

"I'm already in too deep, Lowell. You'd better tell me."

"I will, I promise. I just need another couple of days. I think it's going to happen on Saturday night and that will be a chance to catch the whole gang redhanded, without involving the police." He shot me an anxious look. "It's the way that Mr Avery wants it to be and he's the one hiring me."

I sighed and looked down at Lucky, who was enjoying his newfound crawling freedom in the holding unit I'd placed him in.

"Two more days. I hope nobody else is going to die?" I said, my eyes warning him that he'd better not be playing with people's lives.

Lowell shook his head. "No, this is what they've wanted to hide all along. Everything else was just to divert attention away. It'll be safe unless someone interferes."

"Someone like you," I said with a wan smile, not happy

about any of this. "You know, you really need to give me a better reason than that," I told him, worry creasing my brow. "I know you aren't telling me something vital."

Lowell's answer was to rest both palms on my upper arms and pull me closer towards him. "It will be a huge favour to me," he said, his voice a low rumble.

A shiver ran up my spine and I did my best to cover it up, but being so close to this mysterious man who had been on my mind for more than a week was very difficult indeed. Especially when he seemed fully aware of the effect he was having on me.

"There was something between us the first time we saw each other," he said, his gaze lowered to mine. His right hand moved up and grazed the bottom of my jawline. I tried not to gulp too noticeably.

"If you can't tell me anything important, then tell me this…"

Lowell's expression darkened for a second.

"That tattoo… it's not real, right?" I asked, nodding to the tribal abomination on his upper forearm.

He laughed. It's a fake. I needed something that would make me seem like just another one of the lads. I was hoping they'd be more willing to trust me."

I raised an eyebrow. "And you thought 'tattoo'. That's so inventive."

"Shut up," he told me with a smile, his hand lifting my chin, as he lowered his head to mine.

Our lips met with a crackle of electricity and I fought with my conscience. All of the thoughts about what Lowell was keeping from me spun around in my head for a few moments more, before I slammed the lid down on them. Yes, he was keeping secrets, but right now nothing felt more right than this… this inevitability. Would a few stolen moments really make a difference in the grand scheme of things? It may even make him more susceptible to being grilled later.

I sighed happily as we wound ourselves around each other, forgetting about the troubles of the world for a while.

"Better check on the cow," I said, what felt like an age later. Pangs of guilt had been shooting through me ever since we'd started, and I prayed that Blossom wasn't in trouble. I'd never forgive myself.

I said a little prayer to the god of momentary lapses of judgment and pushed myself up off the floor of the dependent animal unit.

"Can I come?" Lowell asked and I looked at him in surprise before nodding.

"Sure, you're my helper for the night," I told him.

We walked through the quiet night zoo, speaking but not really saying anything. After the brief period of respite, my thoughts were back on the recent incidents at the zoo and everything Lowell wasn't telling me. The more I thought about it, the more I didn't like it.

I stole a sideways look at him, taking in the straight, slim nose and solid jaw line. He may be gorgeous, but that didn't mean I could trust him. I still only had his word that he was working for Mr Avery Senior and that he'd overheard the conversation he'd said he had. What evidence did I really have that showed me he was telling the truth? Was it just another diversion from the truth?

Lowell himself had only turned up at the zoo very recently. That made him a potential candidate for being the animal extremists' inside man. His little 'mistake' on the internet could have been set up to gain trust from anyone curious enough to go looking. Then he'd just spin them whatever yarn he felt he could sell best.

The more I thought about it, the more uncomfortable I felt.

Who was the real bad guy here?

Had I just made a huge mistake and thrown my lot in with the wrong side?

I didn't have too long to ponder. When we arrived at the cow enclosure, Blossom was mooing up a storm and the calf's forelegs were already visible. Then it was all hands on deck to make sure the new arrival was safely delivered.

I kept my thoughts about Lowell to myself.

9

A SILENT PROTEST

"I was so worried about you, and after all that, you were just getting drunk on the sly!" I said to the large fruit bat when I carried her back to the bat enclosure. The air had the tiniest hint of autumn in it this morning and I even shivered when I walked through the zoo beneath the slate grey sky.

Amelie the bat looked up at me with her big brown eyes. I saw no sign of remorse.

After keeping her under observation all night, I'd watched her symptoms clear up, which had given me a hint that the problem was located within the enclosure. A brief inspection of the area had yielded a small horde of rotting fruit, hidden away behind a tree. I suspected this was how Amelie had been getting her kicks. Newly sober and with the rotten fruit all cleared up, I was confident she would make a full recovery.

"Just remember, you lost my respect today," I told her and heard low laughter come from behind me.

Lowell pushed the plastic flaps open and pulled a face at

the warm fug and the smell it carried with it. "You're really telling a bat off for getting drunk?"

"Well, sure. How else is she going to learn?" I said, intending to be funny but finding my words a little sharp. Sleep had not happened last night and it was already starting to bite me in the butt. Not to mention I was seriously peeved at Lowell right now.

"It's almost opening time. If I walk out the back by the cat barn and then back in the front, no one should be any wiser," Lowell said.

I was about to agree when the flaps moved again and Tom walked in. A look of surprise appeared on his face.

"What are you doing here so early, Lowell?" he asked and I felt tendrils of unease spreading through me.

"I just got in early and thought I'd come for a visit," Lowell said, as casually as you like. I was watching Tom's face and for some reason, it looked like that was exactly the answer he'd wanted to hear.

"He stayed the night with me. I asked him to help out because I knew the cow was giving birth and I might not be strong enough to pull the calf out if it got stuck," I blurted.

Tom raised an eyebrow but the sardonic smile never moved an inch. "Why not ask one of the other keepers? I'd have been happy to help," he said.

Now I made a point of looking at Lowell for a good couple of seconds.

Tom raised an eyebrow, his smile becoming more salacious. "Oh, I see. That's going to be hot gossip by coffee time," he said with a chuckle.

I tried not to reach up and throttle him.

"One more thing. On my way in, I heard the builders say there was an intruder last night. They said they met you, Madi, but I don't know if they knew Lowell was here. Did he see anything?"

"Why don't you ask him? He's right here," I said, getting annoyed that I was being forced to speak for both of us. I was just fed up with covering for a 'private detective' who so far wasn't lifting a finger towards digging us both out of this mess.

"Yeah, Madi mentioned it, but I'd walked into town to grab a takeaway. My car broke down, which was the real reason I stayed the night. Well, aside from the obvious anyway," he hastily added. I gave him what I hoped looked like a sweet smile while my eyes told him exactly what he could do with his 'feelings' afterthought.

"Well, that clears up the mystery of why your car was in the car park when the guys left. I think Rich said he was looking for you this morning but if I see him, I'll let him know where you were," Tom said.

I felt chills running up my neck. This whole thing screamed of a set up and I wasn't sure we'd escaped unscathed. The only question was, who was playing who?

Lowell waited until Tom was well and truly out of earshot before he turned to me, his face full of thunder.

"What the hell do you think you're doing?"

"I'm pretty sure that was me saving your bacon, although if this is the thanks I get for saving you twice in 24 hours, I really don't know why I did it. I should have just left you to it," I said, packing the bat carrier away.

Lowell crossed his arms. "I would have handled it."

I raised an eyebrow, unimpressed. "Yeah? They saw your car, Lowell. They're looking for you this morning, so I'd say it's pretty obvious they suspect you. Just, be careful… and, you know, maybe consider telling the person who risked a lot to help you exactly what is going on. Because she might be doubting whether she helped the right person."

"I've already explained all of that. I don't know much more myself and telling you helps no one." He ran a hand through his dark hair and sighed. "I'm good at my job, Madi. You should stick to yours," was all he said. He walked out of the bat enclosure, leaving the flaps of plastic swinging in his wake.

"Well, that was *really* reassuring," I muttered once he was gone.

Tom hadn't been lying when he'd said news of my dalliance with Lowell would be all over the zoo by coffee time. I'd always assumed that because I took little interest in the comings and goings of the other zoo staff, they wouldn't be interested in me.

I was proved wrong.

Perhaps it was because Lowell had attracted his own attention, but I felt like every pair of eyes was on me whenever I passed groups of zoo employees.

I wondered what they'd say if they ever found out it wasn't just Lowell I'd had an encounter with in the last 24 hours. I tried to push away memory of Auryn, while mentally chiding myself for ending up in this situation.

"Should have kept your mouth shut and let Mr Private Detective sort it, just like he wanted," I grumbled to the group of meerkats next to me. It was their turn for a jolly good clean out, but I hadn't selected the best day to do it. Rain fell in fat drops and the clan scattered, diving for their burrows.

I looked through the viewing window and saw Tiff waving from behind three openly staring school kids. Apparently they found me just as fascinating as the animals.

"I knew you were after him," she said to me as soon as I'd extricated myself from the enclosure and the curious gazes of the small people.

"I wasn't after him. It just happened, and unfortunately, Tom caught me out," I said, my voice full of regret. Tiff wouldn't know that what I really regretted, was putting myself on the line for him.

She nodded sympathetically but her smile kind of ruined the effect. "That's so great! He's all muscly and nice. I should get myself one of those," she said with a wink.

I sighed, theatrically.

"Tiff, you've got about ten of 'those' after you at any given moment," I reminded her.

She waved a hand. "You exaggerate." She tilted her head at me and looked thoughtful for a second. "I think someone might be a little disappointed that you're off the market."

"Who?" I said, and then bit my tongue when I figured it out. "Oh, I still don't know why you would think that," I covered, praying that the guilt wasn't written all over my face the way I strongly suspected it was.

"I think I know exactly why I would think that... and you're going to find out for yourself," she said, rather nonsensically.

By the time I'd worked out her riddle, Auryn was already there.

He folded his arms and gave me a hurt look.

"I know what you must have heard but it really isn't what you think, believe me," I said. After this morning, I deeply regretted every second of attention I'd given to Lowell Adagio.

"You spent the night here together. He's not even a zookeeper!" Auryn said, colour rising to his cheeks. "I could have helped you with Blossom. You should have asked."

"I'm sorry. It's no excuse, but everything is up in the air at the moment and I'm not sure of anything, let alone how I feel." I took a deep breath, trying not to focus too much on his perfect skin, or the way his eyes were always full of laughter and mischief - until today, anyway. Was I stupid to turn him down, just because I thought I was more mature than he was? Was it really down to me to decide that?

I mentally shook myself, knowing that a lot of these thoughts had arisen because of the distinctly ungentlemanly manner in which I'd been treated by Lowell. And he was someone who was old enough to know better.

"I meant what I said about proving myself to you," Auryn said, keeping his voice low. "But you can't just..." He trailed off and I felt his pain stab me in the chest. He took a deep breath and his grey eyes found mine again. "A lot of bad things have happened. I don't want you to get hurt by any of it."

"Believe me, I'm trying to avoid that. I don't want you to get hurt either," I said, giving him a smile that he didn't return.

"I guess I'll see you around." He walked away with his head low, his usual vigour absent. I watched him go and frowned as I went over his final words to me in my head. Was it the kind of warning anyone and everyone at the zoo would hand out at the moment, or had Auryn just hinted that he knew something more?

I really hoped I was just being paranoid. At this rate, I'd run out of people I *didn't* suspect of any crime.

The capybaras were next on my list, but before I'd even taken a step in the direction of their makeshift enclosure, I saw Lowell looking at me while he leant against the giant anteater's enclosure.

"Surely you have work to do," I said, not in the mood for anything he had to say after the morning I'd had.

"The legacy likes you, doesn't he?" Lowell said, and I felt my frown deepen.

"That is none of your business, and don't call him that," I said, realising that no matter what Auryn felt, he was still my friend and I stood up for my friends.

Lowell shrugged, that awful tattoo making a brief appearance as it peeked in and out of his shirt sleeve.

"How's the shoulder?" I grudgingly asked.

His eyes flashed with worry and he looked around nervously. I'd already noted that the coast was clear.

"Yeah it's fine. No one's noticed. Other than teasing, I think I'm going to be left alone, so…" he took a breath and made an effort to make his eyes meet mine. "Thanks, for covering for me. I owe you one."

"What you owe me, is the truth," I started to say but had to break it off when we both heard the sound of voices approaching. A group of builders appeared round the corner. Someone let loose a low wolf whistle.

"Leave her alone, we're not paying you to stare at girls all day," Rich said, with a belly laugh that curdled my insides. Blood rushed around my head and with every pump of my heart, I heard the noise of the bomb exploding, again and again. Had Lowell been telling the truth? Was I currently breathing the same air as a gang of murderers?

I gritted my teeth and pushed past it. "Hey, do you guys mind if we chat about the capybara enclosure? I actually wrote down just a few ways that things could be… modified," I said, carefully.

The builders looked at me with all the blankness of sheep. *Good deeds are so easily forgotten*, I reflected.

I bit the inside of my cheek and decided it was time to apply pressure. "It's just, if enclosures aren't built to suit animals, they have a habit of escaping and I might not always be there when they get loose to put them back where they belong." I batted my eyelashes. "And you never know when there's going to be another breakout."

Rich moved a hand up to his scalp. A small bald patch showed where the squirrel monkey had torn out his hair.

"Yeah, proposals. Okay, we can do that." He held out his hand and I pulled a piece of paper from my pocket. Time would tell of course, but I thought I might have finally got my way.

Well done, you succeeded in blackmailing someone who may have planted a bomb. Someone who should definitely be in prison right now, my brain mocked and my brief feeling of success evaporated. Surely this ruse couldn't go on for much longer?

I looked up to see Lowell watching me, his eyes dark with a warning. *Keep quiet.*

Even Lucky couldn't cheer me up when I went to see him in the dependent animal unit. He was much happier with a larger space to explore, and I was pleased to see he was already putting on weight.

"Oh, Lucky, what should I do? I think someone here at the zoo is responsible for a lot of terrible things. " I hesitated. "I'm just not sure who… or even why," I added, admitting my confusion.

I'd thought that the obvious answer was that the people who had planted the bomb, broke into the storeroom, and presumably murdered Ray, were undercover animal rights activists. They might be responsible for vandalising Colin's car and putting up those hateful posters, but they were both incidents that stuck out to me as petty, rather than truly malicious.

If I were to believe Lowell, it would imply that Rich and Co. were an extremist sleeper cell. I frowned and rubbed my temples. Rich had worked at the zoo for years and I'd personally watched him throw rocks at pigeons and yell death threats at the squirrel monkeys. I doubted that was typical behaviour for an animal rights extremist, even while working undercover.

"So what the hell is going on?" I murmured to the little cat, who sighed and fell asleep, his belly full of formula.

Lowell had told me to keep my nose out of the whole business, but there was one suspect I didn't think he'd considered.

It didn't take me long to locate Alison Rowley.

I asked around and was told she was sorting items for the bins behind the shop. I walked down the alley between buildings and saw her crouched down at the end, talking softly to something.

"Alison?" I said, making sure she heard me approach. With everything that was going on, spending time alone in an alley with someone I strongly suspected was involved with the recent goings on at the zoo was hardly a smart thing to do. But I could tell from her voice that she wasn't plotting anything. In fact…

The brown-haired girl turned to face me and I saw a fledgling crow nestled in her hand.

"There's a nest up on the roof, but I think this little one fell. He has all his flight feathers, but there's no room for him to take off in the alley." She walked by me and I followed her to the end of the narrow path. "There you go," she said to the young crow, flattening her palm so it could perch on the edge.

The dark feathered bird shifted its weight from one foot to the other before taking off. At first it grazed the grass, but pretty soon, it got the hang of its wings and was soaring up and up, aiming for a distant tree.

"Is there something I can help you with?" Alison asked, when we'd watched the bird disappear.

I looked at her for a long moment and she seemed to shrink beneath my gaze.

"I'm not here to accuse you of anything, because I don't think you meant anyone harm." I thought about it and realised that was the truth. I didn't know Alison very well at all, but I'd always thought you could tell a lot about a person from the way they treated animals and to all intents and purposes, I believed Alison had a good heart. She just might have taken some bad advice.

"You think I'm one of them... an activist," she said, not looking at all surprised.

"Are you?"

"Not exactly. If you managed to pin down one of the guys out the front of the zoo, they'd tell you I was on their side. They think I'm their inside girl."

She sighed.

"The posters and the spray paint on the car... was that you?"

"I did help organise it, yes." She shrugged. "I care about animals, just like my brother did. Only, it nearly got him killed."

I blinked and looked at her face more carefully, a lot more carefully.

Oh.

"Is your brother Danny Emeridge?"

Alison nodded. "Yeah. He was doing a job he loved, working with animals he adored, and in a single moment it was all taken from him by some jumped up animal rights jerks." I opened my mouth but she silenced me with a look. "Joining them may sound crazy, but I wanted to find out who was responsible for what happened to Danny. The police did nothing, so I was going to make them pay." Her shoulders slumped a little. "I found out a couple of days ago that it was just a couple of thugs who'd joined up when things were hotting up here last time. No one had given them instructions to attack anyone, they just caught Danny out on his own and beat him up for sport. No one even knows who they were," she admitted.

"How come you're still around?" I asked her, and she shrugged.

"It may sound crazy, but I do actually need a summer job. I just got my degree in veterinary science, but I took a gap year, mostly with this in mind."

"Look, I understand your reasons for joining them and I know it was never your intention to harm anyone at the zoo, but did you hear anything about the bomb plot, or plans to break-in, or anything to do with Ray?" I asked, hoping I wasn't making a mistake by deciding to trust her.

She shook her head. "Believe me, if I'd seen or heard anything like that I'd have gone to the police immediately. I know this all looks like some crazy vendetta I had to get even for my brother, and it was… but I'm not a criminal. What I can tell you is that the group of protesters I talk to are baffled. They don't know who planted that bomb or who was trying to break-in. They were shocked when they heard animals might have been poisoned, and horrified when those people died."

"They really don't know who's behind it all?" I asked.

She shook her head again. "Some of them are saying it's a group of extremists. They've heard of stuff like this happening before. That kind of activist wouldn't associate with the likes of us, so no one can say for sure. The rumours are that there's a tight knit group who operate like a terrorist cell. They strike when they think the situation is bad enough to warrant it, but even the people protesting here think it's a rather steep reaction to the death of one animal due to negligence. They thought it was crazy when they were questioned about the break-in and it came out that the police found traces of poison in some of the food meant for the animals." Her dark eyes flashed with fury. "Why on earth would a group of people who were protesting the flaws of poisoning 'vermin' start trying to inflict the same fate on other animals?"

"To prove that the zoo is bad, is probably what the police thought," I said, playing devil's advocate.

I knew what she meant, though. It had seemed strange to me that a bunch of animal fanatics would ever contemplate animal murder.

Someone called Alison's name from the shop and she shot me an apologetic look. "I know what I said about the extremists potentially being here without us knowing, but there's one thing that seems really off about it all." She took a deep breath. "Terrorists, extremists, they all like to take credit for the destruction and havoc they cause. Now… don't you think they've been awfully quiet?"

THE INSIDE MAN

L awrence O'Reilly made his triumphant return to the zoo a day later. He was a member of the board and had been since the days when Mr Avery Senior presided over things. They had a friendship that stretched back for decades and while Mr Avery had finally taken a backseat, Lawrence never left the board. When the bomb went off, he'd been sat next to Mark Sweetly, who was one of the three victims who'd lost their lives.

Lawrence hadn't fared too much better. Shrapnel had torn his face into ribbons and nuts and bolts embedded themselves in his skull and torso. It was only pure luck that had stopped the pieces from hitting anything too vital.

A meeting had been called in the staffroom first thing that morning and we'd been informed that Lawrence was being released from hospital and was returning to the zoo to pay his respects. While there were plans for a permanent memorial to be built for the victims of the blast, at the moment flowers laid outside the closed restaurant were the only signs that something terrible had happened. All the same, I understood Lawrence's need for closure.

It was like having a visit from the Queen. Staff lined up as Lawrence was wheeled by in a wheelchair. He was such a familiar face at the zoo that nearly everyone had words of greeting for him when he passed by. In spite of everything, I couldn't help but smile. Lawrence's return was heartening. It showed that no matter what was thrown at us, we still came back. I wasn't surprised to see Mr Avery Senior arrive, too, flanked by his son, Erin. I briefly wondered where Auryn was, but squashed that little thought straight back down.

"Ooh, isn't he brave," I heard a breathless voice say beside me. I glanced sideways to find that Jenna had arrived. She was clutching her hands over heart and staring with rapt fascination at… Erin Avery.

"It's great that Lawrence is back, isn't it?" I said, hoping against hope that I was wrong about the glaze in Jenna's eyes.

She half-nodded. "Yeah, but it must be so difficult for Erin to come back here. Especially when he so nearly lost his own life. He must be so damaged."

I opened my mouth to say something about it being lucky he'd needed a bathroom break, but Jenna was fully enraptured. I thought about reminding her that he was super old and there was an excellent reason as to why he'd stayed single since his divorce - he was a remorseless workaholic. Instead, I just sighed. I and everyone else just assumed that Jenna would probably learn the error of her ways one day. Until that time, there was no helping her.

"Ah well, at least he's probably still got all of his own teeth," I said, before realising I was speaking out loud. Jenna gave me a very funny look and, to my delight, moved away.

I was about to turn and walk back to the day's tasks when I saw Tom walk up to Lawrence and shake his hand.

"It's great to have you back, Sir. We've all missed you," he said. The keeper of primates looked up and caught me watching. I could have sworn he winked.

Lowell cornered me again when I was on my way out to feed the feral cats. He whistled from inside the same shed he'd once dragged me into. I made a big pretence of ignoring him until I had completed the task of delivering the food. He could stew for a few more moments.

"What?" I said when I returned around the side of the barn and entered the shed. Lowell shut the door after me, but light filtered in via cobweb encased windows and through gaping cracks in the door. I hoped no one was in earshot because this shed was about as soundproof as a paper bag.

"They suspect you're in on it. I can tell. I heard your name mentioned and Rich and the others hushed up as soon as I tried to get close. They think you know too much about their plans," he told me.

I only just managed to not roll my eyes. "I just wish I knew what they think I know. Aside from them being responsible for the bomb, and maybe the other stuff, too, I know nothing. Am I supposed to think that they're secretly a group of animal extremists who've spent years undercover, just waiting for the right moment to strike?" I raised an eyebrow at Lowell but didn't wait for a response. "Somehow that seems like a load of crap to me." Especially when I thought over what Alison had said about the unusual lack of credit taken for the bomb.

"What is this really about?"

Lowell shifted, uncomfortably.

"I came here to tell you to keep out of this, not to drag you further in. Don't you get it? These people are willing to kill for their cause. You do not want to get in the way of that."

I folded my arms and gave him a withering look that would have been way more effective if I were 5 ft 8. "You just said it yourself... I'm already involved. You're not going to the police and from what I can tell, you're trying to handle this on your own. I'm not sure how many people are a part of whatever is going on at the zoo, but its definitely more than one, isn't it? You're outnumbered. You need some allies."

"I'm paid to put my life in danger. It's all in a day's work for me, but you're a zookeeper. I'm here to make this mess go away, not bring you into it," he growled.

"And if they kill you, then what? Everything you've done here will be for nothing. They'll get away with it. Surely it's better to share what you know, so at the very least, there might be someone left who can bring these people to justice?"

"Look, you already know most of what I know. It's the builders who are doing all of the dirty work but there's only circumstantial evidence at the moment. I've got to catch them actually committing a crime. Then I can finally hand everything I have over to Mr Avery and he can do what he pleases with it," Lowell said.

I bristled. "What about the police?"

He just shrugged. "I told you, there's no evidence at the moment other than what I heard the guys talking about. You can go to them if you want but I guarantee, you'll be left all alone at the zoo once the police have investigated. Then where will you be? Even if they did manage to find enough to get the builders, I'm almost certain it goes deeper than that," he said, and I felt a wave of ice wash over me.

"More people are involved in it," I said.

He nodded.

I thought about Tom's interrogation about my relations with Lowell and the way he'd winked at me that morning. Was it because he thought I knew more than I really did?

More to the point, what on earth was this all about? There surely had to be some twisted logic behind the murders.

My heart thudded a little faster in my chest. Oh, this was a dangerous game to be playing.

"How did you know there was going to be a break-in?" I suddenly asked, realising I'd never managed to properly question Lowell after the last time I'd found myself sharing a shed with him.

"I didn't. I just suspected. I was in the staffroom during a coffee break, when a couple of board members were chatting. I think it was one of the men who died and a woman," Lowell said, his face screwing up as he thought back. "It was when the protestors were really starting to get rowdy. The guy was saying, pretty loudly, that he hoped the protestors wouldn't start doing anything like breaking into the zoo and going after food supplies, as it could really make the situation far more dire. The whole building crew were there when he said it. Actually… most of the zoo's staff were in there when he said it, and the guy had a carrying voice."

He shook his head. "Anyway, I made it my business to find out where the food stores were and kept a vigil whenever I could grab a spare moment away from work.

"Then they came and tried to do exactly what the board member feared," I filled in, knowing I sounded incredulous. It just sounded dumb for Rich and Co. to act on something which, to me at least, sounded like a potential trap.

I frowned. "How come you didn't catch them then? That would have been evidence enough."

"I told you, I didn't know when it would happen and before I could get the police in here quietly, you'd already run off to play hero."

I felt colour rising to my cheeks but it soon faded. I refused to let him make me feel bad.

"I did the right thing. If I hadn't gone in and carefully warned them that I was there, anything could have happened. Tom was just a second behind me! He might have surprised them and got hurt, or even…" I hesitated. "Or even taken some poisoned food straight to the animals."

I stopped.

"He's a part of it, isn't he?"

Lowell tilted his head. "I did wonder this morning when he asked so many questions. I figured there had to be other people working with the builders, after all, they don't have much say in what actually happens at the zoo. Zookeepers on the other hand…"

"What are you going to do about it?" I asked, determined to get a straight answer.

"I told you. I need to stick close and give them enough rope to hang themselves with. I've got recording devices on me now, so pretty soon this will all be over. I'll get to the bottom of it and the zoo will be back to the way it should be." He smiled at me but it didn't have the charming effect it might have done, even as recently as last night.

"I think you already know what's going on," I said, moving so I was in front of the door. Sure, he could barge me out of the way no problem, but I hoped I was making a point.

"Fine." He held up his hands and looked exasperated. "Mr Avery noticed that animals who were meant to be shipped both in and out of the zoo have been going missing. No one's noticed, because it's always the excess that goes missing. The numbers at the start of a transfer order start big, but when everything is accounted for at delivery, the number of animals has dropped and the surplus vanishes."

"Someone's stealing animals?"

He nodded.

"That's what Mr Avery thinks. He believes there's some black market trafficking going on. He just wants it stopped as quietly as possible."

I bristled. "They planted a bomb which killed people.

They probably murdered Ray!" I reminded him. "Does the zoo's reputation really mean so much to him that he'd rather hush all of this up for the sake of carrying on as normal? His son is lucky to be alive right now! How can he justify this?"

"I'm just doing my job," Lowell repeated.

I shook my head. "I'm not as precious as you are about my employers. I'm going to the police."

He reached out and grabbed my arm and I looked down at his hand in disgust. He didn't remove it.

"Give me one more night and I swear to you, no one will get away with anything. After hanging around with these guys for so long, I know the signs. I think a shipment is due tonight and it's my best chance of getting everyone that's involved together in one place. Once I'm done, I promise I will do everything in my power to persuade Mr Avery to take all of this to the police." He took a breath. "If he doesn't, I'll do it anyway. You're right. Something like this can't just be covered up for the sake of reputation but I have to get that evidence locked down."

"Then let me help you," I said, but he just shook his head.

"Go home, Madi. Stay safe and all of this will be over by tomorrow." He gently pushed me aside and walked out of the shed into the evening sunshine. I watched him walk away down the trail worn in the grass.

He never looked back.

I couldn't believe how long it took to clear up after the miniature ponies and cows. Hosing down and mucking out was my last task of the day. I'd got stuck in, but it had taken longer than I'd expected.

I took a few extra moments after turning off the hose to

check in on Blossom and her new calf. Now that the challenge of giving birth was over, she and her baby seemed to be doing just fine. The vet was due to come in tomorrow for a check up, but I was confident that nothing was wrong.

"Madi."

I turned and saw Auryn standing by the five bar gate. His golden face had an ashen hue to it.

"What's wrong?" I asked, but he just shook his head, his eyes never meeting mine.

"You shouldn't stay here so late. It's dangerous. You're going home now, right?" he said, and I nodded. Some form of relief drifted across his features. "I'll walk you to your car."

As we were walking, I looked up and noticed the clouds drawing in overhead. The evening sunshine had all but disappeared and by the time we'd reached my car, I could hear thunder approaching over the distant Sussex Downs.

"I'll see you tomorrow," Auryn said.

I watched him, nervously, but he didn't attempt to kiss me again. In fact, it didn't even look like the thought had even crossed his mind.

"Are you okay? You know you can tell me anything," I said, but he just looked at me with his eyes the colour of storm clouds and shook his head once, before walking back towards the zoo.

I drove my car to a distant corner of the overflow car park and left Lucky in his carrier on the back seat. I hoped I would be seeing him again soon.

Five minutes later, I followed Auryn.

The zoo's reception was as silent as the grave. The only sound was the first few drops of rain on the roof, as the clouds released their hold. A glance around the car park had revealed a few cars, dotted here and there, but I had no way of knowing who they belonged to. The only people I could see were the group of protestors to the side of the entrance. They were packing up for the day. On a whim I walked over to them and caught sight of Alison Rowley's brown hair, peeking out from beneath a biodegradable plastic rain mac.

The protestors stiffened when they saw me walk up wearing my zoo polo shirt, but I didn't have time to be berated.

"Alison, can I speak to you for a second?" I asked, already stepping back the way I'd come. The droplets had transformed into a downpour. My hair was soaked and hanging in rat's tails. I hadn't prepared for the bad weather.

"What's up?" She glanced back at the activists, who all had their eyes fixed on her.

I ignored her obvious discomfort. "Something bad is happening tonight. I think the same people who planted the bomb and tried to frame the activists for it are involved."

Alison's expression darkened to match the storm clouds above us. "So, what's the deal? Do you know why they're doing all of this?"

"I think so. One of the builders, Lowell… he's actually a detective. He thinks a group of people within the zoo are stealing animals and selling them on the black market. He reckons there's a new shipment tonight and he's gone to catch them red handed but…" I hesitated. "I don't know, something doesn't feel right," I admitted. Auryn's odd behaviour had tipped me off to that much.

"Have you called the police?" she asked.

"It's pretty high up on my to do list."

She gave me a look and pulled out her phone. After a brief conversation she raised her eyebrows, hopefully. "I don't suppose you're just up for waiting outside until the reinforcements get here?"

I shook my head.

She sighed. "Okay, let's go stop a gang of animal abusing murderers."

"Without getting murdered ourselves," I added. "That would be a bonus."

11

JAILBREAK

I t felt strange to be sneaking through the zoo, which had always felt like home before. Now, every sound made my heart race. The wind picked up, whipping through trees and whining as it rushed through the wind tunnel created by the winding pathway between the enclosures.

"Do we even know where to look?" Alison asked, and I was about to shrug before I actually thought about it.

"Lowell said they were skimming off the shipments. Zoos mostly trade young animals and eggs. I reckon they'll be near the dependent animal unit. That's where most new arrivals go," I said. Despite the probable truth of my deduction, we kept our eyes open and crept through the zoo at a snail's pace. Whilst we moved slowly, we still arrived by the walkway that led to the dependent animal unit far too quickly for my liking.

I risked a look around the corner and saw that the door was open. They were here.

"You just couldn't keep your nose out, could you? What

are you... one of the tree huggers? An animal rights do-gooder?" I heard Rich's raised voice.

The colour drained from my face. I had a shrewd idea as to who he was addressing.

"I just wanted to be a part of what you've got going on. I notice things. I saw you guys always had cash for stuff, so I figured you had something good going on on the side." Lowell's voice was as calm as ever but my own fear levels were spiking.

"You thought spying on us was the way in?" Rich was not buying it.

"Maybe he's an activist, or maybe he's just nosey, but he stuck his nose in the wrong person's business," a voice I didn't recognise said. "Make sure it's dealt with."

"Wait... guys, I just wanted in on the money!" Lowell said. He didn't sound as cool as he had.

"Even if I believed you, you'd still be dead. All Ray Myers knew was that some penguin eggs had gone missing in transit. He didn't really have much of a clue, but he blabbed to Rich and I couldn't risk him sharing his concerns with someone who might actually follow up on it. So, I solved the problem."

"You had him killed, just because he thought some numbers didn't add up?" Lowell sounded genuinely surprised.

"I still don't know who you're working for, and nor do I care, but you have no idea what you've walked in on," the unknown voice said. I didn't like the man's tone. "This isn't just a little bit of pocket money we're talking about here. This is huge. This is the difference between the zoo staying open, or it being shut down and everyone here will lose their jobs. This is the only way to save my family's business," the man said. My mouth fell open in horror. I finally recognised who the speaker was.

"Your father doesn't want this," Lowell said.

Erin Avery laughed. "So, that's it. You're my father's bloodhound. Well, this just proved how out of touch he is when it comes to picking competent employees. Thanks for the tip off. I'll have to figure out a way to make sure he sticks to his retirement in a more permanent fashion."

"Dad, you can't!"

My heart nearly stopped when I heard Auryn's voice. He really was a part of this. He'd known what was happening all along and yet I'd never even considered him until this evening.

I was snapped out of my daze by Alison nudging me in the ribs.

"We've got to do something. The police aren't here and they won't know where to start looking when they do get arrive. Your guy doesn't have long left," she said. Her dark eyes willed me to have a plan.

I stared back at her, my brain feeling as sharp as a limp noodle.

"We need a distraction," I decided.

Alison raised an eyebrow and I nodded, somehow knowing we were on the same wavelength.

"Let's see if the squirrel monkeys are up for another jailbreak."

"How long until the shipment gets here?" I heard Tom ask while we slunk away. The answer was lost to me beneath the noise of the pounding rain, but I knew Lowell was in mortal peril.

It took a lot of persuading to get the squirrel monkeys out of their enclosure.

They were huddled up in their sleeping quarters and despite their natural inclination to get free and spread havoc, they were not big fans of the rain. It was only an inviting trail of fresh fruits that encouraged them to climb aboard before

Alison and I rushed back through the zoo, laden with small, angry primates.

"You know this is a terrible plan, right?" she said, once we were nearly back at the dependent animal unit.

I bit my lip but didn't comment. For all I knew, it might already be too late for Lowell.

I wondered where the police were and figured waiting by the entrance for something to happen would be the answer. At some point, Alison and I were going to have to split up, but right now, getting Lowell out of the hornet's nest was my priority.

A grape and a few strawberries were thrown towards the open door of the dependent animal unit. I tilted my head enquiringly at the three squirrel monkeys, who were clinging to my shoulder. They looked at me blankly.

"Oh come on, now isn't the time to turn *tame*," I said, tipping them forwards. Luckily for me, they went for the food, rather than trying to scratch my eyes out for that little impertinence. I watched with bated breath as they finished the food and contemplated the open door.

"Go on, go inside... it looks warm and you can make so much trouble..." I whispered. We waited another beat and then the lead monkey made up its mind and rushed to get out of the rain. It was all I could do to keep from punching the air as the other monkeys followed. Alison's hanger-ons tore after them,

A shout cut through the sound of the rain and we knew the monkeys had been spotted.

"Get them out, or get rid of them. I don't care what you do. They're worthless," I heard Erin say.

Footsteps approached the open door, heading towards mine and Alison's hiding place. We exchanged panicked looks and scooted around the side of the anteater enclosure, just in time to watch Erin Avery stroll by, his face like thunder.

"Of all the days to be late," he muttered.

He walked off in the direction of reception.

I exchanged a desperate look with Alison and she nodded, knowing exactly what I was asking. Without another word, she slipped through the side gate that led to the maze of paths used by zoo staff. I knew she'd do her best to head off Erin before he could spin the police a line. I only hoped that she'd be able to convince them to come into the zoo and check her story against whatever the son of the zoo's owner claimed.

My life could very well depend on it.

"Get rid of them," I heard Rich growl when I made it back to my listening spot.

"Whoa, hang on a second. I know this is about the bigger picture, saving the zoo and all that, but they're just monkeys. There's no need for us to hurt them," I heard Tom say.

Someone snorted. I thought it was either Todd or Gary.

"We've seen them in action before. It's us or them, and I choose us. Don't go developing a conscience now. It was your idea to feed the serval that poisoned rat and leak the info when the boss said we needed to get the protestors riled up. You were the one who sweet talked Lucy into telling you which cat would be dumb enough to take any extra food offered," Rich said.

"Yeah and I still feel like a giant jerk for that, thanks for asking. I'm also glad I was stopped before I could get that poisoned animal food. Come on, man, these little guys have names!"

"And I have a machete. Big deal," Rich said, and I heard the sickening sound of a blade thunking into something solid.

"You missed!" Tom said, his voice full of horror. "I always

knew you were a psycho, Rich. This is so messed up." He sounded like he was realising it for the first time.

I had zero sympathy for him.

An outraged screeching broke out and I realised I couldn't remain a passive observer any longer. It may not be the rescue mission Lowell needed, but I couldn't let anything bad happen to the squirrel monkeys I'd put in danger. I was furious with myself. Of course a gang of criminals would carry weapons around with them!

"Stop what you're doing right now. The police are already here." I boldly stepped into sight.

Six pairs of eyes looked back at me.

Auryn's face was drawn and pained when we made eye contact for the briefest of moments. Lowell's was the mirror image with a trifle more exasperation thrown into the mix. Tom looked shocked, but Rich seemed more amused than angry.

"Deal with it," he said with a cruel smile, directing his words at Tom and Auryn. I saw Auryn shake his head. He backed away from Rich, just as I turned to sprint.

There was the sound of more screeching and the patter of small paws. The squirrel monkeys shot back out into the rain and I was glad of the added confusion. I needed every second of my head-start. Whilst staying on my feet all day kept me in pretty good shape, with my small stature, I was hardly a world class sprinter. Getting caught was an inevitability. I just needed to put it off long enough.

At least, that's what I told myself.

I had no idea if what I was doing would buy enough time for the police to get in here and save us all, or if they were even going to make it past the front gate. If Alison had been caught by Erin before she'd made it there then we were all dead.

I looked back over my shoulder and saw Tom was

starting to gain on me. Although he held a machete in his hand, it didn't look like he was particularly trying to catch me.

"Come on, Madi, let's work something out. You can be a part of this and help save the zoo! That's what really matters, isn't it?" he called, his voice still steady and even.

"You killed people!" I shouted back with much less composure. My sprint had faded to a slow jog, but Tom still hung back.

"I never killed anyone. The bomb was Gary, and it was never meant to be that big. He nearly blew up Erin, who genuinely was saved by a call of nature. We had been planning he'd just stick around at the back of the room and let some dust ruin his suit for authenticity, but Gary screwed up big time," Tom said, starting to pant a little now. I looked back and noted he was only a couple of steps behind me.

Running suddenly seemed kind of pointless, so I stopped.

Just as I'd hoped, Tom didn't immediately brain me with the machete.

"Rich was the one who did Ray in. Ray told Rich when he noticed something off about the penguin egg order. I guess he thought they were buddies." Tom shrugged. "He spotted that the numbers on the order were too high but by the time he got his hands on the eggs, there was exactly the number he'd ordered in the first place. Rich told him to talk to Erin about it, figuring he'd think of something to shut him up. But we all know Ray wasn't great at keeping a secret. Erin said we couldn't risk him telling anyone else." He scratched his neck, thoughtfully. "Looking at the evidence, I think it might have already been too late to stop that."

"He told Mr Avery Senior. That's why Lowell was brought in. Mr Avery's known all along what his son is up to," I concluded, suddenly feeling far less charitable towards old Mr Avery. He'd suspected what was going on and hired a detective to make sure, but even when all fingers pointed in the direction of his son, he hadn't gone to the police. It was true what they said about being blind when it came to your own family.

"What gave you the idea to pin all of this on the activists?" I asked, figuring talking was better than dying.

Fortunately, Tom didn't seem keen to get down to business either.

"When those thugs attacked the old apprentice, Danny, and everyone just pinned it on these unknown guys who were working with the animal activists, it got Erin thinking. The police went after the attackers, but because they were involved with the activists, he said their whole investigation was skewed. The cops couldn't do much more than ask if anyone knew who the thugs were. The activists closed ranks and said they didn't have a clue and the police didn't want to push beyond that. They'd risk bringing the wrath of all activists down on them and all sorts of dirty words like 'discrimination' would be thrown around." He grinned and I shivered.

"Erin thought it would be a great safety blanket. All we had to do, was stir up the animal rights groups, so that they targeted the zoo. That's why he pushed for rat poison and got me to throw one to the serval. It was the perfect cover we needed in case any loose ends needed to be tied up. We knew the police wouldn't look too closely because they're so afraid of disturbing the activists." He sighed. "It hasn't exactly been a blast though. No one was ever supposed to die."

"But what about the animals you're selling? What happens to them?" I asked.

Tom shrugged. "They're fine. It's all private collectors who can't get the animals they want anywhere else. We're not even taking much of a risk, as we only pass on animals there are a surplus of in zoos - like the penguin eggs. They're pretty much impossible to get hold of as a private collector, but pretty damn easy for us. Our buyers pay big bucks, we get a bonus and Mr Avery pockets the profit and folds it back into the zoo, out of the kindness of his own heart."

"You really believe that?" I asked.

Tom nodded, his grip shifting a little on the handle of this machete. "Sure, it's no secret that this place costs a mint to run. Entry prices have been raised but they did a load of market research and experts figured out that there's an upper limit to what you can charge. People stop coming after a certain point. What's been happening is that the zoo looks as successful as ever, but the money coming in has stayed the same while the cost of running the place has gone up. If you don't believe me, just look at how slow the directors have been, replacing the two keepers we've lost. That's no coincidence."

"What you're doing is wrong, Tom, you know that. I saw you just now when Rich wanted to kill the squirrel monkeys. You care about this place as much as any zookeeper who works here. Surely you realise there's got to be another way? Most businesses can be made to work more efficiently and improve their profits. They don't automatically have to turn to something illegal to keep things going," I said, and for a moment I really thought I was getting through to him.

"Can't trust you to do a thing," Rich said, appearing around the corner of the meerkat enclosure.

Tom looked at me, indecision written across his face.

I saved him the trouble of deciding by punching him on the nose.

He bent double, clutching his bleeding nose and swearing. I wasted no time finding out how much damage I'd really inflicted and ran for it. Man-mountain Rich barrelled after me.

My heart nearly burst out of my chest when I saw a blue uniform.

I looked up at the young female police officer who was reaching for her baton. Her eyes were uncertain when she saw me tearing towards her.

"He's got a knife, look out!" I yelled, opening my palms to show I wasn't the one armed. Rich gave a bellow of rage which drew a male officer out from a side corridor. His hand was wrapped around the upper arm of Alison Rowley. My heart sank at the sight of their surprised faces. This wasn't the big rescue I'd envisaged.

"These two are insiders working for the animal rights activists, please arrest them." Erin Avery said, stepping out from the same corridor that the male police officer. He was followed by the Detective Rob Treesden, who had recently been spending more time than ever at the zoo.

"I'm a zookeeper here, not an animal rights activist. The man you are standing next to is responsible for the murder of Ray Myers, the attempted poisoning of animals at the zoo, and the planting of a bomb which resulted in the deaths of three people," I said.

There was a stunned silence as the police officers vainly tried to work out who was telling the truth. The machete bothered them. That much I could tell.

"If you don't believe me, go down to the dependent animal unit and you'll find a private detective, Lowell Adagio. He's been restrained and told he's going to be killed for investigating their black market animal selling business," I carried on.

At least... I hoped that was what they'd find. Hopefully I'd been enough of a distraction for Rich and the gang that they hadn't got round to carrying out their threats.

My eyes met Erin's washed out blue pair and I thought I saw the first traces of doubt creeping in.

"This is a simple misunderstanding. I asked Rich here to cut back some undergrowth that was getting in the way of the new enclosure and he volunteered to stay behind to do it. I'm sure he was surprised by Ms Amos here, which is why he's still holding the garden tool." Erin did his best to pour reassurance and authority into his words, but even he couldn't spin this story to his advantage.

"Contact Mr Avery Senior, the zoo owner, if you need even more proof. He's the one who employed Lowell to investigate his own son," I said.

That seemed to be the grain of sand that finally tipped the scales in my favour. The lead detective pulled out a radio and messaged for back up. Erin Avery just kept staring at me before he must have realised he was about to lose everything.

"You're really taking the word of an obviously distraught employee over the head of the board of directors? This is a waste of police time!" he protested, but this time he wasn't listened to.

"It's our duty to investigate these claims, sir. Once we have looked into it, we will make our judgement," the detective explained.

Everyone seemed to have forgotten the fact that Rich was still holding a machete. Erin made eye contact with him and the head builder made to lift his blade, only for all three officers to raise their batons. For a moment, I wondered if Rich was going to attack anyway and damn the consequences, but he relaxed his grip on the machete and it clanged to the floor.

"I just did what he told me to," Rich muttered.

I exchanged a relieved look with Alison Rowley when the police officer restraining her released her arm and walked over to Rich instead.

It wasn't long before the reinforcements arrived and we made the journey to the dependent animal unit. Auryn had got into a fight with Todd and Gary and all three were looking rather worse for wear, although happily no machetes had been brought into play.

"They were going to take him to the penguin pool and push him in, still tied up," Auryn muttered to me while the police arrested Todd and Gary. They hauled Lowell back up off the floor from where he'd presumably been knocked over during the fight.

"I'm sorry I didn't tell you. I didn't want any part in this but dad said I had to do it. I had no idea they were behind the bomb, and Ray..." He gulped. "I only found that out this evening when they told me I had to help them out with this shipment. I swear I didn't know much at all, they kept me out of it. I just thought it was something a bit illegal on the side." He shook his head and his floppy blonde hair curled down over his eyes. "I guess I was so worried about fitting in here and doing my part for the family business that I didn't see what was really going on. I'm so sorry it nearly got you killed."

A police officer was watching us. He tilted his head at me in a silent question. I sighed and turned back to Auryn.

"You'd better go with them and give a statement. Tell the truth and it will be okay. I know you weren't really a part of all this," I told him, figuring it was the best I could do. I doubted any charges would be made against him. It was as plain as day that the poor teenager had been co-opted into this mess. I believed him when he said he hadn't had any idea of the lengths his father was going to. Perhaps to an outsider, it may seem obvious, but just as Mr Avery Senior had proved when he hired a private detective instead of going straight to the police, love for your family could make you blind to their flaws.

EPILOGUE

I t was quite a surprise to think that just three weeks later, you wouldn't have known anything major had changed at Avery Zoo. Mr Avery Senior had stepped out of retirement and promoted his old friend, Lawrence, to joint head of the board of directors. They had acknowledged the deficit that Erin Avery had been covering up and were working on ways to get the zoo's coffers back in the black.

One of the new ideas that had been announced was a greater focus on environmental impact and education. Apparently there were a lot of grants and funding that could be applied for and the board were hopeful that the zoo could be saved simply by investing in the future of the planet.

Rich, Gary, Todd, Tom, and Erin, were all awaiting trial for various offences including murder charges. I'd heard they were out on bail, but a restraining order had been put in place to keep them away from the zoo. The police offered me protection on the off chance that someone wanted to get even but I'd politely refused. It might seem naive, but I felt like it was over. The fake extremist group had been used to cover things up, but with everything out in the open, it was my view that they wouldn't be out for revenge. It had never been that personal. The whole operation was about money with some extreme, and not always intentional, collateral damage.

I spared a thought for poor, unfortunate Ray, whose only error had been confiding in the wrong person. I wondered when Erin Avery had decided that saving the zoo was worth more than a man's life? The thought had probably never crossed his mind when he'd told Rich what to do. Killing Ray had simply been the path of least resistance.

When the news had broken at the zoo, I'd briefly become a celebrity. Everyone wanted to know exactly what had happened that stormy night when the squirrel monkeys had mysteriously escaped again. I hadn't helped to further the gossip and was always careful to avoid mentioning Auryn whenever I was forced to talk about it.

Auryn Avery had been let off with a caution. The police had concluded that he'd been forced to join the group and had no knowledge or involvement of the depths that his colleagues and father were willing to sink to. Since then, I'd noticed him spending a lot more time with his grandfather and I was pleased that instead of tearing the family apart, the traumatic events had brought them closer together.

Now almost four weeks old, Lucky's eyes were open and he was starting to explore the world a little more. I'd also noticed a couple of tiny white teeth poking through soft pink gums. My little kitten was still wholly dependent on me but he now spent every day in the dependent animal unit until home time. I popped in for regular feeding and cleaning, but I had helpers in the form of multiple zoo employees who'd cottoned on to Lucky's existence. I'd managed to keep Lucky's brothers and sisters (who were doing just fine) a secret, but in truth, I was glad that so many people were involved with Lucky's care. It was just another thing that brought those of us who worked at the zoo closer together. I hoped it would serve as a reminder that we were supposed to be like a big family. We'd all seen firsthand what happened when people forgot that.

Lowell had turned up at my house bearing flowers a week after he'd been rescued from near-certain death. The fact that it had taken him a week to come to terms with needing to be rescued, and that there was someone he needed to express gratitude to, didn't surprise me one bit. I just told myself that at least he'd acknowledged it in the end. Perhaps he wouldn't be so willing to dismiss help when it was offered in future cases.

The most challenging thing that had happened after the night when Erin Avery et al. had been arrested, was having to round up the squirrel monkeys the next morning. The rain had passed on and after a night of freedom, the monkeys had not been keen to return to their home. Catching them was made especially hard due to them being pretty sick and tired of even the juiciest summer fruits. I only had myself to blame for their overindulgence but with Tom under arrest, it had once more fallen to me to try and persuade them to come back home.

To my surprise, after the news of the night's events had spread, half the staff had turned out to herd the monkeys back into their enclosure. We'd managed it in record time with only one person getting bitten (me).

A new group of builders had hastily been hired to complete the capybara enclosure, and due to their lack of a track record with the zoo, it wasn't too much of a challenge for me to shoehorn in the changes I'd lobbied for all along. Doris and Louis were now back in residence and I was pretty certain they'd never looked happier.

Another group of new additions were the four zookeepers brought in to replace Ray, Colin, Tom and Lucy.

Lucy had left after news of Tom's involvement broke and she must have worked out how she unwittingly aided in the demise of one of the animals she was so dedicated to looking after. After having your trust broken like that, I couldn't blame her for not wanting to hang around a place where you'd constantly be reminded of your mistake. It was a big personnel change and had taken some getting use to. Things had calmed down when the rota had been drawn up, although I still found myself pleasantly surprised to find I now had time for a lunch break.

With the summer just starting to fade, the only dramas now were the ones which unfolded daily when working with animals that made such hilarious fodder for my webcomic. I smiled and remembered my surprise on Monday morning when I'd woken up to no less than ten fan emails. My comic's views were doubling every week and it just made me happy to know that there were people out there sharing the moments I found funny.

"God, you need a boyfriend," Tiff had said when I'd told her all that. Perhaps in the past I'd have agreed with her, but after my recent experiences, I was willing to wait a little longer.

I sat down on a rock and watched the two echidnas bustling about in their enclosure. It was a year since they'd had their new arrivals and while litters remained rare in captivity, I had everything crossed that they would surprise us all again with some brand new puggles.

A flash of blonde caught my eye. I looked up and saw Auryn leaning over the side of the enclosure. I smiled at him and hoped it didn't look forced.

After he'd been released by the police, we'd had a long discussion about everything that had happened. He was incredibly broken up inside about it and I was so angry at his father for forcing him to be a part of the scheme. No part of me blamed Auryn (a young man who felt like he had so much to lose and even more to prove) for being coerced. The problem was, I knew that he still blamed himself and that was something I couldn't change. I could tell him I forgave him a thousand times, but until he forgave himself, things would be different between us.

It was probably for the best, I reflected, as I exited the enclosure and walked around towards the front to meet Auryn. His feelings for me had made me question my own for him and left me with a lot of doubt over what it meant to do the right thing. Now all we had to focus on was rebuilding our friendship.

"How are things?" I said, once I was next to him.

He looked over the enclosure for another second and I did the same, both of us watching the echidnas squabbling over a pine cone.

"Things are okay. Grandad's asked me to sit in on the board meetings. I think he's serious about training me up to take over the zoo some day," he said.

I looked at his face carefully but could read no signs. "That's a good thing, isn't it? You've always wanted to work at the zoo."

"I did. I do," he hastily corrected, and a rueful smile appeared on his lips. "Yeah, it is good. It's just... unexpected. I always thought I'd have years of dossing around and training to be a zookeeper and then one day, in the super distant future, I'd run this place. You know, after I knew, like, everything about everything. The way adults do," he added.

I choked noisily. I was glad when it made him smile.

"Believe me, that illusion is well and truly shattered," he admitted. "Anyway, now it's like, all rushed. I think I could be in charge of a lot of things in just a few years' time. Grandad was meant to be retired from all of this stuff and now he's had to come back in and promote Lawrence, too. I don't mean to be morbid, but they're not exactly young and I'm scared that..." He paused. "Well, I'm just scared, I guess."

I tilted my head at him, feeling an unexpected sense of pride wash over me. "That's exactly the attitude you should have, so don't worry about it. If you thought it was going to be an easy ride where you can do whatever you like without consequences, well, that's when things go wrong." We exchanged a look, both of us thinking about Auryn's severely misguided father.

"The most important thing for you to remember is that you aren't alone. Even when you do take over running the zoo, you have so many friends. If you ever find yourself struggling, or in need of anything, all you need to do is ask and I guarantee you'll discover that so many people want to help you," I said.

I was pleased to see the worry lines fading from his forehead. I wasn't here to sugarcoat anything for him. He was going to have some tough times ahead, if the zoo fell to him before he was ready - which it undoubtedly would. But he was already so much more of a man than his father had been. With the attitude he was displaying, I sensed that Auryn Avery would be the kind of man who shone instead of crumbling under pressure. I was looking forward to seeing where he took the zoo.

"Oh, I can't believe I forgot to say. I actually came here to let you know that Grandad wants to see you."

"Do you know what it's about?" I asked, immediately curious.

"No, but he's been singing praises to your heroism since the day it all happened, so I don't think it'll be anything bad. Maybe you're getting a medal or something." He smirked and I felt a brief return to the easy friendship we'd once had.

"Great. I've always thought that what this uniform really needs to set it off is a medal."

Despite my joking around, I was actually very curious as to why Mr Avery wanted to see me.

Along with Alison, I had been instrumental in ending the black-market animal trafficking at the zoo, but considering that the ring leader was Mr Avery's son, I hadn't really expected much thanks.

I told myself it was paranoia, but I did wonder if I was about to get fired. I couldn't exactly think of a good reason, but what if old Mr Avery wanted to start completely fresh and my face was the one that reminded him of the bad times?

I mentally shook myself when I approached the main office. Speculating wasn't going to help. I hesitated with my hand poised in front of the heavy oak door. Then I knocked.

"Thanks for dropping by, Madigan. Please have a seat. I've been wanting to catch you for a while," Mr Avery said. I perched nervously on the edge of a black leather armchair, feeling like I was attending an interview.

Still rifling through papers on top of his desk, Mr Avery seemed completely unaware of my discomfort.

"Yes, I was going through all the records and so on after…" He cleared his throat. "Anyway, I found quite a few letters regarding you."

He looked at me over the rims of his glasses and I knew surprise was written all over my face.

"So, this is the first you've heard of it, eh? I thought as much." He nodded to himself. "These letters are from various zoos and and institutions of animal care." He fanned out a bunch of them. "Some quite impressive places, too. They all wrote to commend you for the work they say you've done with various breeding programmes. Specifically highlighted, is your success with understanding echidna breeding habits, although other achievements were also noted."

"That's… really nice of them to say so," I said, pleased but baffled as to why this warranted a trip to the office.

"Yes it is, isn't it? They didn't write to merely sing your praises though, as charming a habit as that would be. They're actually all enquiring if you're available for habitat redesign and breeding consultancy. That sounds pretty fancy to me." He raised a bushy white eyebrow. "I think what it means is they all want you to do some work for them, and seeing as the word 'consultant' is batted around, I'd say there's some good money in it, too! Now, what do you say to that?"

I sat there stunned for a few seconds, wondering if I was being encouraged, or accused.

"That would really interest me. Making sure the animals I look after at Avery Zoo are in the best possible environment we can give them is what I love most about my job," I cautiously ventured.

"Now you have a chance to do the same thing for zoos all over the country." He flicked through the letters again. "Actually, even outside of the country. So, would you like to do it?"

"But I love working here," I said, feeling torn by the choice I'd had thrown in my lap.

"I know you do, believe me, I can tell. You've done more than enough to show that." He let it sink in for a moment. "You wouldn't be leaving your job here. You could come and work whenever you don't have consultancy clients. We'd have to get another zookeeper in to cover you permanently of course, but what I'm saying is, you could be our consultant, too." He put both hands on the desk and leant forwards. "Now, I have no doubt my accountants would say I'm crazy for offering opportunities like this and letting irreplaceable staff walk away, but I think this is what is best for both you and the zoo. You'll get to make a difference doing what you love and are best at, and Avery Zoo will benefit from having a reputation for excellent animal care and knowledge. In my books, that means everyone is a winner." He sat back again. "I think that is far more important than hiding things like these letters away and hoping that we can cling onto you forever. What do you say?"

"I'd love to," I said, feeling excitement dashing through my veins. It was like being offered my dream job as a zookeeper all over again - only even better.

Mr Avery smiled over the rims of his bifocals.

"Excellent. Well, there's a zoo in Little Edging, Shropshire, who seem to think their meerkats are clinically depressed and their emus hell bent on homicide. I recommend you start there. Always start with the hardest tasks first. They're the ones where you'll find out what you're really made of."

I nodded, hardly able to think over the fizzing in my brain. A group of animals who needed my help beckoned and I couldn't wait to get started!

EXCITING PREVIEW!

Read on for an exciting preview of the second book in the Madigan Amos series, The Silence of the Snakes!

THE SILENCE OF THE SNAKES

12

PROLOGUE

Darkness was an old friend to the man dressed in black. He slid between shadows, blending seamlessly with the exotic shrubbery which bordered the manicured lawns. On the brow of the hill, Dracondia Manor looked down on its domain. A few lonely lights still twinkled at windows, but it didn't concern the man in black. He knew that the lights probably belonged to those long since travelled to dreamland. People who feared the dark.

He nearly pitied them.

A peacock cried out as he was crossing the paving slabs, but he didn't flinch. No one had their eyes on the man using the servant's entrance to get in. He reached the simple oak door and pressed down on the latch. It swung open without so much as a squeak and beneath his moustache he smiled. The one element he had left to chance had worked out and had it ever really been a question of chance when he'd offered that kitchen lad a whole Crown for his trouble?

The man wet his lips with his tongue as he silently stalked the empty corridors. The kitchen boy had also been kind enough to advise him on the best route, but he wasn't fool enough to take too much for granted. Instead, the man had found the original building plans and meticulously plotted his route from there. Only when he was sure he knew the inside of Dracondia Manor as well as any servant did he make his move. And it would be this patience that yielded the prize of a lifetime.

He walked through corridors so silent he could hear his own heartbeat in his ears and climbed up narrow staircases that any person of breeding wouldn't countenance setting foot on. Darkness and silence had always been his companions but even he was beginning to feel it turn oppressive. The shadows were starting to move in front of his eyes and his muscles were tensed to jump up and run. The man took a couple of deep breaths and realigned himself before pushing open the heavy, carved double doors.

Although he couldn't see it, he could sense the particles of dust swirling around in the large room. The air felt thick and heavy, as though no one had been here for a long, long time. Another thief might have begun to doubt, but the professional had done his research. He knew that it was here.

He walked across the vast rug, stepping over the swirling pattern. If he'd been more observant, he might have noticed that the undulations of the pattern were unusually random. The tip of every swirl had a yellow circle embroidered on it, completed with a black strip of thread down the centre. It had the uncanny effect of making it appear as though the rug was always watching whoever walked across it.

The man's attention was elsewhere. Next to a grand piano made from flawless ebony, an ornate walnut table stood proudly next to it. There, at the centre of the table, was the priceless Serpentine Emerald.

He moistened his lips again and strangely felt rather scornful. The gem he had poured so much of his patience into stealing was left out on a table, like a common ornament. He reasoned that it could be there to deliberately mislead the casual thief, who might overlook it as a shiny rock. Or perhaps the owners of the emerald believed the stories about the jewel being cursed. He nearly chuckled aloud. They were fools like everyone else if that was the case.

Ever since the term 'treasure' was coined, he reckoned that the stories of terrible curses attached to such items had existed. People liked to believe that there was some magical power at work that kept shiny things in the hands of their rightful owners, and brought the wrath of hell down on those who dared to steal. His moustache twitched up as his lips curved into a rare smile.

They were all wrong. The only real curse was that of a poor thief who got caught and sought to blame his incompetence on a piece of jewellery. It did make for some good stories though, he allowed, as he stretched out his hand and plucked the jewel out of its stand. His fingers spasmed for a moment and he only just avoided dropping it. A dull pain throbbed in his wrist and he was reminded of his ever advancing years. It was just as well that this was his last job. Turn the emerald over to his unscrupulous buyer and a wealthy retirement beckoned.

A narrow stream of light suddenly showed beneath a small door in the far corner of the room and the man felt a jolt of raw panic snap through him. How could he have been so careless to stand around mooning at the emerald, contemplating his retirement? Hadn't he always said that it was celebrating success too soon which got good thieves caught? Now he was about to fall prey to the same flaw he'd criticised.

By the time the door swung open, the man in black was already concealed within the heavy, velvet drapes. If he were a child, playing hide and seek, he would be caught in seconds. All he could hold onto was the hope that no one was looking for him. He tightened his grip on the large emerald and prayed that its disappearance would also be overlooked at this late hour.

That was a more dangerous roll of the dice.

His heartbeat seemed to double and then treble as he listened to the sound of footsteps walking around the room. Sometimes they came so close, he was sure they were only inches away, separated by the luxe fabric. Were they toying with him? He wondered, as sweat started to pour from his brow. He was really panicking now and he knew it. Behind the heavy velvet curtains it got harder to breathe every minute and there was a strange metallic tang in his mouth. Any moment now he would pass out and fall to the ground, revealing himself and the emerald to whoever had interrupted him.

And then they were gone.

The man in black wasted no time breathing a sigh of relief. As soon as the light had faded and the footsteps were no longer audible, he slid out from behind the drapes. His normally light footsteps felt strangely sluggish as he stepped back across the unusual rug and eased himself back through the double doors. Back in the silent darkness, his heart continued to race. Another bead of sweat joined the steady stream running down his temples and he tried to shake himself out of it. He'd nearly been caught. So what? It had happened to him a thousand times. Admittedly, not recently, but he could forgive a little drama on his last ever job. It would be something to tell the kids about. Or it would have been if he'd ever found another human tolerable enough to spend long enough with to warrant children.

It was only when he was once more in front of the small oak servant's door that he finally admitted to himself that something was wrong. His limbs were shaking uncontrollably. It was a supreme effort just to keep the emerald fixed in his slippery palm, but he never took his eye off the prize until the job was done. Too many riches fell from pockets during hasty exits.

I must be coming down with something, he thought, as he stumbled through the door. He hardly winced as it banged against the stone wall - a mistake he would normally have found unforgivable. He didn't care anymore. All he wanted to do was get home and get to bed, so he could ride out whatever this thing was.

The black spots started appearing in front of his eyes when he was only a quarter of the way down the garden. The man who'd slid from shadow to shadow now staggered across the lawn like a local drunk. His heartbeat kicked up another gear and he felt certain it was simply going to explode any second now. He fell to his knees as the black spots turned to arctic white and he lost vision, collapsing onto the dew kissed grass.

He barely heard the laughter of the man who walked towards him. He felt the kick, though - swift and painful to his left ribs.

"There are always thieves who want to try their luck with the Serpentine Emerald. Don't you know it's cursed?" he said.

The man on the floor moaned. It was the only sound left to him.

"Now, I'm sure you think you're a smart man. You don't believe in curses, but you should have believed in this one." He knelt down and listened for a moment to the strains of increasingly laboured breathing. "The curse is real you know, but it doesn't have a thing to do with the emerald." He grabbed hold of the man's legs and dragged him, semi-conscious, across to the centre of the lawn, directly beneath the imposing glare of Dracondia. "And everything to do with me," he finished.

With one swift movement, he kicked the dying man off the ledge and into the circular pit. Far below, the black mambas hissed and struck at the unwelcome new addition. Their fangs pierced skin, injecting their deadly venom straight into the veins of their victim. The thief made no move to fight back. He was already dead.

Lord Snidely pulled a handkerchief from his pocket before he bent down and picked up the Serpentine Emerald. One side of his mouth twitched up as he listened to the enraged hissing that emanated from the pit of snakes. It sounded like scalding water spilling out from an overheated pot.

"I really must get around to fencing that off one of these days. It's just an accident waiting to happen."

PAWS AND CLAWS

I pointed to the litter tray and then back at Lucky. The five week old black and white kitten tilted his head, quizzically.

I sighed. "I suppose it's just as well we spend most of our time outside."

After I'd been persuaded to leave my job as a zookeeper at Avery Zoo and become an animal welfare and breeding consultant, I'd taken bookings for zoos with animal problems - problems I specialised in solving.

My first ever job at a zoo in Shropshire had turned out not to be the challenging case I'd been expecting from their initial plea for help. Once I'd arrived at the zoo, it had been clear that the aggressive emus and the depressed meerkats were suffering from the same thing - a lack of stimulus. It was a simple matter to pen some brand new enclosure designs and also suggest plants, toys, and creative challenges for the animals to complete to receive small, food rewards. The zoo had been pleased with the progress that they'd immediately seen, and my second job had already begun.

Things had moved so fast, I'd barely had a moment to reflect back on what had happened at Avery Zoo.

Avery Zoo's troubles had started when a serval had died after eating a poisoned rat. Then, I'd been the unlucky person who had found the penguin keeper's body at the bottom of the penguin pool.

Things had gone downhill from there.

In the end, the truth about the goings-on at Avery Zoo had come out and I was still counting my lucky stars that I'd managed to avoid the same fate as the penguin keeper. After a change of zoo management, it had been brought to my attention that there were other zoos who'd heard of my success with Avery's breeding programme. The zoo had been home to several animals who rarely bred in captivity. My greatest success was with the echidnas.

My secret? I thought it all stemmed from being able to understand animals' needs. You could tell a lot from an individual's behaviour, and I also knew that the habitat provided made a world of difference. At Avery Zoo, I'd made it my mission to make sure every animal in my care was as happy and healthy as she or he could be. The results spoke for themselves and it had been enough to get me noticed by other zoos. That was when the owner of Avery Zoo himself had suggested I become a consultant. I still retained my ties to Avery, but now I travelled around, working with different animals and solving their mysteries to give them the best future possible.

My second case was an interesting one. Snidely Safari and Wildlife Park was, for all intents and purposes, your average British animal park. I was already finding it fascinating working with the larger animals that hadn't been present at Avery Zoo. Snidely had lions, tigers, gorillas, elephants, giraffes, and many more besides. I had been tasked with reviewing every single group of animals and submitting a report on my findings to the owners of the safari and wildlife park.

But the job had one twist I wasn't as confident about. The safari and wildlife park was not the only place that housed a large collection of animals. Dracondia Manor, the residence of the Snidely family, was partially open to the public. What made it a shade different from your average historical Manor was the large collection of reptiles and amphibians it housed. Most notably - snakes.

The Manor's slithery inhabitants had been included in the job request, but I was already finding them a challenge. Every zookeeper has their specialty and mine had been, well - anything with fur of some kind or other. I also had a fair amount of knowledge of birds, having cared for them when the resident bird keeper at Avery Zoo had taken a holiday, but snakes were something I hadn't really encountered and didn't know nearly enough about. I had explained all of this to my new employers, but they hadn't seemed to take it to heart. They'd assured me they expected me to report on all of the animals. The objective was to come up with a review of current animal welfare levels, suggestions for improvement, and then to lead a discussion on what to do moving forwards.

I could understand why the Snidelys wanted one person to do the whole job, but it meant I was going to have my work cut out for me. On the plus side, my employers hadn't given the job a deadline, and it was an excellent opportunity to expand both my animal knowledge and my resumé. I also had a secret plan for how I was going to be able to give feedback on Dracondia Manor's cold-blooded collection. The Manor was a draw for reptile enthusiasts the world over. I'd already written and placed a questionnaire for visitors to the Manor to fill out, which included asking for suggestions for improvements to the reptiles' enclosures and care.

Sometimes I surprised even myself.

I pushed my glasses a little higher up my nose. Today, I'd worn a red-rimmed pair to try to add a splash of colour to my otherwise English rose face and short, overly wavy blonde hair. I also hoped the glasses would draw attention away from the army of freckles that had invaded my face. It was the price I paid for working outside during the summer.

The printer in the little office area I'd been given coughed to life and spat out a piece of paper. I surveyed the worksheet I'd created that would enable me to give a standard report for every enclosure.

I'd been at the zoo for a week. In that time, I'd already completed my review of many of the more familiar animals' enclosures. The wild boar and ponies, who roamed the wildlife park with a giant gathering of deer, had needed no further comment from me. However, I did have a problem with the deer. They were quicker and bolder than their counterparts and - frankly - greedier.

To encourage animal engagement, Snidely allowed visitors to buy cups of animal feed to pass out to the animals in the wildlife park on their drive through. It hadn't been hard to notice that the deer had been the main recipients. They were all fat. I was suggesting a review of the food given to them. Instead of pellets, perhaps vegetables and popcorn could be mixed and given.

I snorted at the thought of putting an entire herd of deer on a diet.

Lucky started meowing and kicking up a fuss to let me know he was hungry. I obligingly poured him out a bowl of milk formula. He was just starting to get the hang of drinking out of the bowl, although I thought more milk ended up around his mouth than in it.

"Isn't it great that we get to hang out together all the time now?" I said to the little kitten, who continued to stuff his face. One of the benefits of labelling myself as a consultant was that I got to make a few rules of my own. Lucky was a non-negotiable part of the Madigan Amos consultancy package - not that anyone had complained so far. That was the benefit of working at zoos - they were pretty accepting of animals.

"Well, Lucky, I'm off to see some of your bigger cousins," I said to the black and white kitten. He yawned luxuriously and nearly fell asleep in his milk. It was a cat's life all right.

I popped him back into his basket and made sure I shut the office door behind me. Lucky had just begun to explore his surroundings and I definitely didn't want him wandering around - especially in a place that specialised in snakes! Even a kitten as lucky as Lucky could come unstuck if he met one of them.

If I were being really honest, I was worried about coming unstuck myself.

Dracondia Manor's collection stood out from every other zoo's for one reason - the reptiles and amphibians they kept were all venomous.

I drove a little way off the main track in the lion's enclosure and killed the engine of my Ford Fiesta. It didn't exactly blend in the way one of the safari's zebra striped vehicles would have done, but the Snidelys had suggested I use my usual car for two reasons. The first was so that I wouldn't be bothered by any members of the public asking questions, and the second reason was that all of the animals reacted to the striped vehicles. They knew it meant food was on the way and my review of their natural behaviour would be skewed if I turned up in a familiar vehicle.

A people carrier stuffed with children slamming their

hands up against the windows passed by. The parents threw me a dirty look out of the window, probably thinking I was being reckless by breaking the rules and driving off the designated track.

At least, that's what I assumed, until they turned off onto the grass and drove closer to the pride of lions I was currently observing.

I waved to them through my windscreen, motioning for them to return to the track. In return, they flipped me a rude gesture, and I saw their kids howl with laughter in the back. To my horror, the back window rolled down and a child leaned his elbows over the glass. A horrific news story in which a person had been wrenched through the window of a car and torn to pieces by a lion flashed through my mind. Left with no other choice, I rammed my hand down on my horn, sounding the alarm.

I only hoped it wouldn't be too late.

One of the young adolescent males had stood up when I'd beeped my horn. I watched as he lifted a paw and glanced at me before turning his head in the direction of the people carrier. The child wiggled his hands in excitement. I felt a bead of sweat slide down my back. Were his parents crazy? Their child could be moments from death!

My hand had migrated to the car door handle without my noticing. I looked down at it and then back out at the lion. His posture had changed and his ears were flicked forwards. The raised paw dropped and he lowered his body, slinking forwards. It didn't take a genius to realise he was stalking the child. Unfortunately, his parents were apparently as far from geniuses as you could possibly get. The father was snapping photos on his phone of the approaching lion, while the child continued to shout and wave his arms - or lion tooth picks, as they were about to become.

I swore under my breath and pushed down on the door

handle. Despite it definitely not being my fault that the parents had so foolishly decided to leave the track and then let their kids run wild, I couldn't help but feel a little responsible for them deciding to drive off the road in the first place. Perhaps riding around in a stripy jeep was a better idea after all.

The lion didn't even look round when I opened the car door and stood up on the grass. I kept a close eye on the rest of the pride (who were mostly asleep) and banged as loudly as I could on the metal of the door. The stalking lion jumped and looked my way, his eyes meeting mine over the top of the car door I was currently shielding myself with.

He shook his burgeoning mane and turned back to the easier target of the child.

"Shut your window, or you'll die!" I shouted as loudly as I could.

Perhaps it wasn't the best choice of words. Instead of closing the window, the child looked at me and froze, his elbows and upper body still hanging out of the car. The lion sensed his distraction and launched forwards.

I prayed for a miracle.

There was a 'phht' sound, and the lion jerked away from his killing run. He jogged to the side, lashing his tail and trying to bite his shoulder. A few seconds later, he fell to the ground with the feathered tranquilliser dart still sticking out of his side.

I looked towards the track at the black and white stripy vehicle and breathed a sigh of relief. Kerry, one of Snidely's big cat staff, looked pretty relieved, too. She'd evidently been driving along with the regular tourists, on her way to investigate the horn blast. I couldn't blame her for the less than urgent response. People accidentally hit their horns daily, but on this occasion it had been an emergency. I was just grateful that she had arrived in the nick of time.

The parents had finally realised what had almost happened. The child had been dragged back in and the window wound tightly shut. The people carrier started to move back towards the track, but the big cat keeper wasn't finished. The zebra jeep swung off the track and revved its way across the grass before neatly swinging round in front of the people carrier, forcing the driver to slam on the brakes. The angry father opened his window (apparently forgetting everything that had just happened) and waved his fist, shouting obscenities.

Kerry remained in the jeep and turned on the loud-speaker system. I couldn't help but smirk when she drowned out the man's yelling with her reprimand. She informed the parents of the very real danger their child had been in and when the man dared to gesture towards my own car, Kerry jumped on that, too. She told the irresponsible pair that I was a member of staff, and even if I weren't, one person breaking the rules does not mean you should do it, too. Honestly, it sounded like the sort of speech you'd expect to be giving to children - not their parents.

After she'd finished up and let the driver get back to the track, she drove the jeep over to my car and parked close next to me. I scooted over to the passenger side and we both opened our adjacent windows, close enough together that no lion could get in between.

"Can you believe I just had to do that?" Kerry said, her bleached blonde hair escaping from her plait. She looked across at the dozing pride of lions and shook her head. "Unbelievable. It's made me come over all strange. When Orlando made his move back there, my heart, it just..." She mimed a rapidly beating heart with her hand.

"Sorry I caused you trouble," I said, knowing I'd done nothing wrong but still feeling responsible. "Will Orlando be okay?" I asked, nodding my head in the direction of the knocked-out lion.

"Yeah, he'll be fine. As soon as we're out of here, I'll get a team in to make sure he's okay and that the needle comes out. They'll be able to do it safely." She blew air out of her mouth and shook her head. Her eyes widened and she lifted a hand to her temple. I suddenly noticed it was slick with sweat.

"Wow, I guess the stress of the situation really did get to me." She giggled and then looked horrified for a second before giggling again.

This time she didn't stop.

"Kerry, are you oka-"

Before I could answer the question, she threw open the driver's side door. It hit my car door with force and I knew there'd be a big dent. "Hey!" I started to say, but she carried on giggling and stepped out of the jeep. As soon as I saw what she was doing I tried to get out myself, before realising her door was blocking mine from opening. I beeped my horn again, desperately hoping she wasn't the only keeper in the vicinity, but it was more than likely.

"Stop, Kerry! What are you doing? You can't just walk out there!" I shouted out of my open window when she passed beyond the relative safety of our parked vehicles.

I watched, frozen in horror, as she walked around the side of my car and continued towards the pride of lions.

They didn't look so sleepy now.

One of the lionesses saw her approach and grunted.

Kerry was still 15 metres away from the pride when she collapsed.

I kept staring at the spot where she'd gone down before I finally comprehended what had happened. The big cat keeper had just passed out in front of a group of curious lions. I swore and looked around in vain for the second stripy jeep I was hoping was already on the way.

Nothing appeared on the horizon.

The lioness pushed up onto her paws and stretched - just the way a regular cat does when it wakes up. Her ears flicked forwards and she looked over at the spot where Kerry lay still in the grass.

"You've got to be kidding me," I muttered, realising that the cavalry weren't coming this time. I was the only person who could do anything to avert disaster.

BOOKS IN THE SERIES

Penguins and Mortal Peril
The Silence of the Snakes
Murder is a Monkey's Game
The Peacock's Poison
A Memory for Murder
Whales and a Watery Grave
Chameleons and a Corpse
Foxes and Fatal Attraction
Monday's Murderer

Prequel: Parrots and Payback

A REVIEW IS WORTH ITS WEIGHT IN GOLD!

I really hope you enjoyed reading this story. I was wondering if you could spare a couple of moments to rate and review this book? As an indie author, one of the best ways you can help support my dream of being an author is to leave me a review on your favourite online book store, or even tell your friends.

Reviews help other readers, just like you, to take a chance on a new writer!

Thank you!
Ruby Loren

Death's Endless Enchanter

Death's Ethereal Enemy

Death's Last Laugh

Prequel: Death's Reckless Reaper

BLOOMING SERIES

Blooming

Abscission

Frost-Bitten

Blossoming

Flowering

Fruition

Made in the USA
Columbia, SC
20 February 2018